MW01253481

Neither Here Nor There

stories by MARCEL JOLLEY

Joe,
Thanks for your
great books &
your encouragement

Black Lawrence Press
New York

Black Lawrence Press
Brooklyn, New York
www.blacklawrencepress.com

Cover photo: Jason Smith
Design: Sarah Crevelling and Colleen Ryor

ISBN 0-9768993-3-7

"Neither Here Nor There" was published in a slightly-different form in *The Portland Review Literary Journal*, Volume 50, Number 3, Summer 2003.
"Archenemy" was published, also in a slightly-different form, at *WriteThis.com*, Volume II, Issue VII, February 2005.

This is a work of fiction. Any resemblance to actual persons, living or dead, or events is entirely coincidental.

Contents

FOREWORD

Marcel Jolley's imaginative scope can be wonderfully clear, and yet mysterious at the same time:

I am, for the most part, unremarkable. I am twenty-six years old, a conservative thirty pounds overweight, and I work as a clerk for a well-known chain store offering copying, printing and binding services. The company prefers "copy artist," but in the interest of honest self-appraisal, I decline the title. I hail from Beaverton, Oregon, a collection of Olive Gardens, Red Robins and Pier One outlet stores interchangeable with countless other parasitic suburbs riding the coattails of better-known cities. Combine this heritage with a 2.7 undergrad GPA and half a master's degree from a state university and my milquetoast normalcy solidifies. I have something, though, that sets me apart from most people, an ace up my sleeve. I have an archenemy.

What impresses me most here is the author's ability to create a very distinct parable form in the grey formless world of American suburbia. The voice is clear, but the tone has distinct strangeness to it. There is humor, but also a bit of darkness in its foretaste. There is obvious self-irony, and yet also a touch of unexpected pride. Jolley gives us very routine American characters and conversations while still charging them with a sense of the unknown.

And here are also a few voices we may already know:

"Yo!"
"Yo, Jade," I say. "It's Casey."
"Hi, Casey. This isn't Jade."
"Okay."
"Wanna take a guess?"
"Not particularly."
"You are no fun," she says, and I can't argue.

And—

"Say hi to Mike for us," Dad says.
"Is he still with that girl?" Mom says.
"Yes, he is."
"I was never really sure about her."
"I'll pass that along," I say. "Love you guys."
"We love you, son."

We know these sorts of conversations. We have them ourselves. These familiar everyday voices fill Jolley's stories because they allow him to make the darker mysteries of the human psyche seem comfortable to us, if only for a moment. He gives us pictures of dumb, boring, blank days spent in copy stores or at bars with former college buddies. And yet, on the same page, he also shows that the most mundane, brainless activity can be wonderfully interesting and spiritually satisfying if it is observed with enough human interest, empathy and attentiveness.

Jolley may be observing the ordinary surfaces, but his concern always lies with the core. He is interested in the mysteries of identity which both reveal and betray our very inner desires:

"My archenemy senses me coming and looks up. His eyes betray the smallest amount of concern. He knows this is not my stop. He knows something is happening. He knows who I am."

Luckily, Jolley's search for identity is filled with narrative pleasures and urgent plots. There are characters who "drank a few beers, but they might as well have been a church group. Everything was 'yes, ma'am,' or 'no, sir.' They kept completely to themselves. They'd done things, you could tell." We meet a neighbor who tells high tales of murder and intrigue, and we meet unrequited lovers. But most of all, we find in this collection the music and promise of the narrative that is simply captivating:

As a result, I threw my twenty-five year old life into my twelve-year old car and descended from Mile High City. The car always knew where to go before, so I trusted it again. It deposited me in Bozeman, Montana, home of my alma mater and several friends who long ago eschewed degrees for season passes at Bridger Bowl. I was there with no definite plans to leave when my parents called last weekend with news of my friend's death.

And so the journey begins. Fasten your seat-belts, dear readers, for *Neither Here Nor There* is the best sort of adventure in fiction—it finds a way to make the most unassuming things strange and wondrous by the means of its attentive and muscular prose.

Ilya Kaminsky
San Francisco

For Cathy

...and I remembered something you once told me,
And I'll be damned if it did not come true,
Twenty thousand roads I went down, down, down,
And they all led me straight back home to you.

Return of the Grievous Angel

NEITHER HERE NOR THERE

Everyone in town claimed to know someone who drowned in the channel. Maybe it was just rural folklore, or perhaps with a year-round population of five hundred, everyone had simply known the same drowned person. Despite these warnings, local kids still spent summer days out there watching the tides whip in and out in flurries of white water. At night teenagers drove there to drink, fumble their way toward sexual prowess, and take the hairpin turn at the channel's edge as fast as their old cars and young nerves allowed.

The tide's movement through the channel was violent and fascinating. Local fishermen blamed ghosts from sunken boats, a few Tlingit old timers spoke of angry spirits, and smart college kids up for the summer used terms like "venturi" and "Bernoulli's principle." Whatever the reason, watching the channel's stagnant pockets and seaweed-covered rocks fill and empty with a river-like rush had the feeling of something meant to be. You knew it would keep happening whether or not anyone was there to watch.

The four boys arrived after noon, fresh from baseball practice, and dropped their bikes beside the dirt road. The one named Danny led the others over the rocks and down into the tide pools. He wasn't so much big for his thirteen years as he was substantial. A large ribcage gave him a head start and the Tlingit blood from his mom's side added an angular strength. Already he sprouted natural patches of muscle that the other three would later spend fruitless afternoons on the high school's worn Universal set hoping to replicate. Behind him walked Casey, taller than Danny but lanky. His awkward movement suggested an extended break-in period lay between that afternoon and the time when he would feel comfortable in his own skin. The other two boys, Mike and Dustin, followed closely. Both were interchangeable with each other, if not a million boys worldwide. They were good boys who would grow into good men, reliable and predictable. They would always buy the table a round at their turn and would return borrowed tools in good condition and a timely manner. They all followed and Danny led with the same reluctant ease with which he would lead them to a 2A Division basketball championship four years later.

The tide was out and the channel empty save for a few bigger pools. The rocks were as dry as they would ever get, but still slick underfoot. Seaweed and mussels hung everywhere in dirty clumps, waiting for the water's return. It would come soon. The boys knew this, in the way most kids from Southeast Alaska possessed some innate sense for water. They played among the tidal pools, searching for any sea life trapped there by the previous tide's rapid departure. They found only the standards—diminutive starfish, kelp and jellyfish parts.

"Jim Tully claims he found a sea otter out here last month," Dustin said.

Mike agreed. "I heard he was gonna keep it, but it got free on the way home."

"He also said he got his hand down Sandy Nelson's panties," Casey said. "And she gave him a shot to the nads for it."

They all paused, waiting for Danny to chime in. He stood watching the first trickles creep into the channel's far end. He cocked an eye and gave them what they wanted.

"Tully's full of shit, that's for sure."

And that was that about Jim Tully, his sea otter and Sandy Nelson's panties.

The channel would fill soon. Danny led the others back up over the slippery rocks onto the dirt road. Each boy grabbed a length of leftover kelp on the way and a spontaneous battle erupted. They whipped each other to welts until the kelp strands cracked and popped apart in their hands. They laughed and performed damage inspections of each other. The water rivulets swelled down onto the rocks at the channel's far end, growing thicker.

The boys perked up their ears, listening for cars roaring down the dirt road for a sliding ninety-degree turn at the channel's edge. They scanned the waters outside the passage, searching for local boats. They spoke of the money older brothers and cousins earned and how they themselves would be out there at their first chance, maybe just another couple summers. Danny talked of the late 60's muscle car—maybe a GTO, maybe a Mustang—that his fishing money would bring to town. Danny didn't say it but the others knew his first order of business would be the channel road. They would all be riding along, taking the corner faster than any of them wanted, scared to death. Knowing this made them enjoy that quiet, dry summer day a little more.

They were just leaving when Casey heard the cat. He started talking louder in hopes no one would notice the mewing and they would soon be on their bikes headed home. But Danny heard, just like Casey knew he would.

Dustin spotted the cat first, across the channel from them. It must have crossed earlier at low tide and now started down below the waterline to return. The cat wore a collar and telltale bell, but Casey didn't recognize it as one of the town's familiar pets, such as old man Field's one-eyed tabby or the Jenkins' three-legged Hopalong.

Mike threw the first rock, sharing with Dustin the nervous chuckles of conspirators with no definite plan. The rock landed well right of target, a dull ricochet off a thick patch of seaweed. The cat's tail ballooned and the animal crouched lower, awaiting the rocks that both the cat and the boys knew were coming. Dustin and Mike plucked and threw rocks quickly, their efforts proving why they were relegated to first and second base. The rocks came nowhere near the cat, but rather sent the animal on a sporadic course around the seaweed and tide pools. Realizing their limitations, the two soon decided it wiser to use their poor aim to keep the cat in the channel until it filled with water. Knowing the others were eyeing him, Casey picked up an oblong rock and threw it lazily. He hoped to land a few strategic shots forcing the cat to the other shore, but he was a catcher and had the worst arm of the four.

A thick preliminary stream coursed down the channel, drawing from the healthier pools. The cat leapt over the stream only to land in a large puddle. It sprung out, soaking wet and suddenly skinny, and headed for the opposite shore.

"Shit, it's getting away," Mike said. They redoubled their effort with renewed vigor and failing accuracy.

Danny took two steps to his left and picked up a rock, rolling it from hand to hand. The other boys stopped their throwing and watched. Whatever would happen was now going to happen. Whether or not they wanted it, whether or not Danny wanted it. Even the cat, still picking its way over the wet rocks, appeared to sense the futility and slow its flight.

Danny rolled the rock into his throwing hand and cast a quick glance to Casey, his catcher. As with his glances from the mound, Danny looked less for agreement than forgiveness, an okay from a friend to go ahead and use his natural gift. At the ball diamond that look apologized to the sub par player who stood between them at the plate, whose parents sat in the stands watching Danny strike out their son. Today his glance apologized to whoever owned that cat, the people who would spend the next few nights searching the woods outside town and hanging handmade missing posters on telephone poles and the post office bulletin board.

Casey gave only his usual non-committal nod of a friend. He knew Danny would throw the rock and hit the cat. The stone would kill or at least stun the animal until the water filled the channel, like it had yesterday and like it would tomorrow, and that would be that. All this would happen regardless of whether ghosts, angry spirits or just basic science was to blame.

I read somewhere once how two in the morning is the midnight of the soul. Crossing the Columbia River near George, Washington at 2:17 a.m., I understand the sentiment. I've traversed a time zone since leaving Bozeman this afternoon and worry I've somehow forced my soul to linger even longer in this shifting midnight. After a day of turbo-flavored chips and 32-ounce sodas, my soul is probably used to the abuse.

Souls aside, these are desperate traveling hours. I see only the headlights and taillights of people rushing to get to their destinations before their trip and its dubious motives are exposed to daylight's unforgiving scrutiny. What would an inspection of these cars reveal? Absconded children or goods, bail money, or maybe just fingers crossed in hopes of finding the car in a new and better place when it finally stops. A green Ford Escort hums by on bald tires. Inside sits a lone skeletal blonde with a death grip on the wheel. She stares straight forward as if she just caught first sight of Seattle's lights, still two hours and a mountain range away. The Escort's right side is severely dented and damaged. When this woman wants to go right, she goes right. I slow to give her a wide berth.

My own motive for late night travel is the archenemy of desperation—complete freedom, or darn near it. My only appointments are with Alaska Airlines for a flight north to Juneau in two days, and after that with an old friend, now dead and waiting for me and several others to put him in the moist Southeast Alaska ground. A grisly appointment indeed, and one I would avoid had I anything—a job or prospect thereof, a girlfriend, or even oral surgery—to cite as an excuse. I have nothing. I lay claim to only a 1980 Datsun B210 and a life that fits in the back with room to spare.

Until last month I worked as an engineering analyst for a well-known defense contractor. Among the red rocks of the Rocky Mountain foothills outside Denver I fine-tuned minor systems on missiles. Like most who worked there, I convinced myself my work and research was not of the nature that directly blew people up. Someone there apparently did do work of that nature, because just over a year ago the products of my company and our competitors put on quite a show on CNN and created a one-month war. The missiles proved so efficient that many minor players like myself received our walking papers. The young lady I was seeing at the time didn't want to ruin my streak and also sent me packing, ending our seven-month run over bottomless steak fries at a Red Robin off I-70.

As a result, I threw my twenty-five-year old life into my twelve-year-old car and descended from the Mile High City. The car always knew where to go before, so I trusted it again. It deposited me in Bozeman, Montana, home of my alma mater and several friends who long ago eschewed degrees for season passes at Bridger Bowl. I was there with no definite plans to leave when my parents called last weekend with news of my friend's death.

Three o'clock finds me standing outside a gas station mini-mart in Ellensburg, bathed in the glow of a sign claiming twenty-four hour service. Everything indicates life. Neon lights emit an artificial hum, all things microwaveable wait in a plastic case to be unwrapped and devoured, and the hot dogs and sausage links inside roll toward me on their metal treadmill but grow no closer. The doors, however, are locked in a blatant disregard for company policy. The clerk is no doubt engaged with a joint, a girlfriend or a magazine, but my near empty gas tank demands I await his return.

I walk to a nearby payphone, pull a (206) number from my pocket and dial it. Thoughts that those awaiting my arrival—a life-long friend and his Bellevue girlfriend—are sitting at home quietly concerned as to my whereabouts are dispelled when the receiver is lifted. The background of music and laughing rises first, then a voice jumping in like a wet t-shirt contestant.

"Yo!"

"Yo, Jade," I say. "It's Casey."

"Hi, Casey. This isn't Jade."

"Okay."

"Wanna take a guess?"

"Not particularly."

"You're no fun," she says, and I can't argue. First comes a thump, and I worry my fun deficiency has gotten me hung up on. Then I hear a chuckle and a grasp.

"Where the hell are you, Casey?"

"Hi, Jade," I say. "I'm getting gas just outside Ellensburg."

"All right." Her tone wavers. She is one of thousands of Puget Sound girls who attended the U of W or Western in Bellingham and returned to Seattle via some homing instinct. To her kind, anywhere east of Snoqualmie Falls is like side two of the Nirvana album she bought for the first song. She knows it's out there, but by that point she's not listening anymore.

"About an hour and a half," I say.

"But the party will be over by then."

"Can I come anyway?"

"Of course, sweetie. You can sleep in and we'll take you around town tomorrow. I bet you want to talk to Mike."

"If he's available."

"Anything for you." I hear a hand palm the receiver for a moment.

Then: "Hey, bud."

"Sounds like I'm missing all the fun," I say.

"I suppose." I visualize Mike dragging a disappointed look over the remnants of a good time crowding his apartment. "A couple of Jade's friends came over. Trent and Kelsey, I don't think you know them. They just got back from hiking around Thailand and we've been looking at their pictures and tying one on. So you'll be here in a couple of hours, huh?"

"'Bout that, I guess."

"Cool," he says. "So when is your flight on Wednesday?"

I decode his message. "So you're not going?"

Mike exhales and launches a practiced defense. "I can't, Case. We've got a big project going up in Mountlake Terrace and I really need to stick around. Jade's dad is having me head up the whole thing."

I toe the dirt beneath the phone. "I got you, pal. That's okay."

"Yeah, so anyway." Mike clearly welcomes the passage of this exchange and moves on quickly. "Hey, check this out. I talked to Dustin the other day. He said Brad Mullen had his boat outside the channel that morning and saw a pod of killer whales out there."

"Huh." I spin on a noise behind me. The lost clerk has resurfaced. The pudgy and badly-complected young man unlocks the doors with an embarrassed smile hinting his reasons for being AWOL are less than admirable. With surprisingly succinct hand and eye gestures, we wordlessly agree I need pump number one on and I am to pay inside.

I retake the phone. "Kinda early in the season for them, huh?"

"Exactly," Mike says. "I remembered that legend we studied in Mr. Scott's Alaskan history class, the one about how a killer whale showing up means the spirits are coming to take someone away."

"Yeah," I say. "But, I think that was a Chugach legend. Danny was Tlingit, and only half at that."

"Oh yeah." A sad chuckle follows. "Maybe the whale couldn't tell the difference. No. No, that's bad. I shouldn't have said that."

"Ah, don't worry about it." I hadn't noticed. I am only thinking how proud the now-retired Mr. Scott would be of our last exchange.

"Yeah, Case, I feel like shit about not going to the funeral, but there'll be plenty of people there." Mike pauses. "You know Kristen's going, don't you?"

I hear the pump kick on and light up. I shiver and tell myself it's a result of the cold.

"No kidding? When did you hear from her?"

"She lives here, dude, in Seattle," Mike says. "I ran into her a few weeks ago at Southcenter. She moved up from San Francisco and is living with her aunt here. She called the other day to see if we were going, and I told her you would be there. I think she's even on the same flight to Juneau as you. Her and the German guy, y'know..."

"I heard."

"So, yeah, she got custody of the little boy. He was with her, real cute. Her hair's a little longer, little more brown, I guess."

Mike has found his trump card for bowing out of the trip and earned his release.

"Well, Mike, I better hit the road."

"Okay, buddy, we'll leave a key in the planter."

"See you soon."

I hang up and suck in a noseful of chilled air ripe with the aroma of a hundred cows awaiting a dubious future back off I-90. It stinks and sends pinprick aches down into my lungs, but it's all right. I am energized. Mike gave me what he knew I wanted—an actual sighting with seemingly insignificant but telling details and hints of inevitable future contact. I pump gas and think of questions I never could have asked Mike. How much longer was her hair? How far had it strayed from the stylish bi-level I'd always wanted to run my hand through? How did she react when he mentioned I would be at the funeral? Was her German clothing magnate trying to win her back, in whatever way a clothing magnate did that?

Riding close behind these musings is a comfortable futility, one that in the end kept me sane during my school years alongside Kristen. I dislike the term "crush" and never found a suitable synonym, though I guess in a certain way I could have been labeled a "Kristen enthusiast." I was akin to a sedentary sports fan, cheering my team on over beers and hot wings, stretching logo-laden apparel to its extreme with my undisciplined bulk. Any chance of getting in the game myself was doubtful, and if given the opportunity, an embarrassing defeat seemed imminent. Such was my hopelessness that even close friends couldn't bring themselves to tease me. Instead they broached the subject like a hobby I persisted in despite no promise of a pay-off. Like stamp collecting, maybe, or oboe lessons.

Despite the sincere sweetness Kristen had always exhibited toward everyone, her romantic future always seemed to lie on a horizon beyond the mountains of Southeast. Save for a few elementary school steadies, Kristen never dated anyone from town. She opted instead to see college guys during the summers and had to finally venture overseas to Der Faderland for a suitable spouse. Despite that union's demise, it still doesn't give much hope to someone she has known since grade school who now probably feels to her as comfortably familiar as a parent's old coat.

Still, as I merge back on to I-90 with my fellow desperate travelers, I think how I wouldn't have expected Danny to be dead barely eight years after our championship game. Time passes and things can change. I feel momentarily guilty for the morbid hope I gain from this, but in a car with a failing heater, I can use it for warmth.

Danny always put scars into two categories. They were a by-product of either bravery or stupidity, though both often sprung from the same well. Whenever he assessed his own collection, from the crooked line under his elbow to the nickel of tissue on his left knee, he figured he just about broke even.

None of his past wounds, though, boasted the texture of the one sliding under his fingertip. Rough but rhythmic, it read like a Braille curse word. Marlene, the scar's owner, shifted under his touch and didn't even lift her head from the pillow.

"Knock it off."

She sweetened this with a smile, understanding his need to touch. Though Danny didn't bear the scar nor did he want to, he felt it his right. Responsibility granted a certain ownership.

"What's it been, two years?" he said. "You healed up real good."

No response. Marlene was asleep again.

They had been drinking heavy that night out at the channel, like a hundred times before and a hundred since. Driving back Marlene was hanging out the passenger side of his Chevelle, her full weight pressing her hips down against the half-open window. The others followed in Jim Tully's truck, and Marlene was flipping them the bird or flashing her goods or something like that. Sometimes Danny could convince himself he never noticed the pothole in his headlights. Other times he knew he saw it coming. The door window shattered, cutting right through her 501's. The glass sliced a five-dollar bill in her pocket clean in half and damaged a big muscle with a Latin name, but just temporarily. Now that night remained only as a ribbed snake crawling from her right hipbone down to where her business started.

The remainder of Marlene's hip shone pale white, it being only April, and hinted at a few stretch marks. Danny eyed the scar one more time and pulled up the sheets. He lay beside her with his eyes wide open. The clock read 6:15. He could normally sleep until nine, but a temporary stint tying lines for the state ferry at all hours had messed with his rhythms. The job ended last week but he still couldn't sleep right. He looked forward to the steady tempo of the coming summer, maybe even a nice easy charter boat job.

He forced himself to sleep another hour and a half but finally couldn't take it. Marlene awoke only when he jingled his Carhartt jacket to ensure his keys were inside.

"You can use my toothbrush if you want," she said.

Danny slipped on the jacket. "That's okay."

"You've had two root canals, mister. You can't go too long without brushing."

Danny only smiled. The awkwardness of these mornings after was long gone, but he still wouldn't admit he spent enough nights here to promote tooth decay.

"Well, shit," Marlene said. "I guess I'm hungry, then."

She pulled a Hawaii '88 t-shirt over her head and stood, allowing Danny just a hint of the scar and its accompanying flank. He had seen Marlene naked more times than he could count, but damned if watching her cross the tiny one-bedroom apartment didn't put a little lead back in the pencil. She pulled out some Frosted Flakes and put a bowl down for him.

"Sorry, it's all I got. I need to hit the market today." She grinned. "I wasn't expecting company."

Danny took a seat with Marlene and looked out the apartment's lone window. Perched atop the hardware store, her shoebox apartment allowed a view of the three-block downtown as it sloped down to the docks and the bay. Usually a person could see the round green mountains rising across the water, but this morning only a mean multi-layered fog hung out there. No mail planes today.

"It's Tuesday, isn't it?" he said.

"All day, boss. Any big plans?"

"Never."

She leaned across the counter and put a cassette in the

little boom box on her windowsill. The apartment filled with the grating noise of some has-been hair band—Def Leppard, maybe, or Whitesnake—the tape's case long lost and the titles worn from the plastic after too many handlings. The tape may very well have been Danny's copy, though it would have been years since he missed or looked for it. Marlene took his right hand, again examining the swelling around the knuckles. Danny instinctively acted as if it didn't hurt.

"Poor baby. You've got to be more careful."

He let her continue caressing his hand. "Hey, basketball is like that. You fall down."

"A good turnout?"

"The usual. Enough for a couple of teams."

"Was Bobby there?"

Marlene slipped her fingers fondly to his palm. He suddenly wanted her to stop.

"I think so. It's open gym, y'know. People come in and play and leave. I can't remember everyone."

She increased the pressure on his palm. "I hear he's a good ball player. For a kid, I mean. I just wondered what you thought."

Danny pulled his hand back. It wasn't sore anymore.

"He's okay, I guess. For a kid. He still coming in while you're working?"

Marlene stirred her Frosted Flakes, letting the sugar soak into and sweeten the milk. "Yeah, he and the other school kids hang around while I'm closing and cleaning up the tables. I mean, there's nowhere else open and nothing to do that time of night. It's just a little crush, if that. It's kinda sweet, I think."

Danny's bowels groaned as her glam metal crap started into another song. He wanted to throw the boom box through the window, but settled on just turning the volume down.

"How can you listen to this stuff in the morning?"

Marlene shrugged. "I like it."

"You do know there's been music put out since 1987?"

She only smiled at him and lifted her bowl to sip the sugary milk. "Sometimes it's nice just to know the words."

He couldn't argue. Danny stood and jingled the keys in his pocket.

"I'm going by the post office. Got anything to mail?"

Marlene put her bowl down and grinned like she would for a puppy. When she stood, her arms wrapped inside his jacket.

Her t-shirt radiated warmth. At five foot two, she only came to his sternum and when he breathed deep her fingers barely touched across his back.

"You've got the greatest build," she said. "This big damn ribcage. Have I ever told you that?"

Only every damn time they hooked up. She was right, though, and he viewed downplaying it like refusing an inheritance. Danny's frame had always been an athletic barrel, making his upper body look bigger and more substantial. But his physique was a simple gift and that alone. He didn't consider it his to mess with or alter, just like the small ring of softness that only recently began straining against his tucked-in t-shirt. He knew no amount of exercise would do any good. It was all just part of the ride.

He held her a few seconds more, never sure of their non-committal embraces. He searched for just the right caress and pressure to ensure her door would be open the next time he called, but not so much that she would think them more than just old friends with compatible loneliness and body parts.

"I better get going," he said, and she let him drift away. The tape in the boom box stopped with a loud click.

"So I go in at about four today," she said, crawling back under the covers. "I don't know what the specials are but I'm sure Jimmy will whip up whatever you want."

"Maybe," Danny said. "I might go over to my parents. We'll see. Anyway, you got any mail?"

She pulled the blankets up and pointed innocently at the fridge. Two stamped bill envelopes hung from a salmon magnet, one for her visa and another for Alaska Power & Telephone. He pulled both down and pocketed them.

"You're a sweetheart," she called from the bed as he opened the door. He leaned back in for one last look, letting the day's first chill into her doorway.

"Don't let it get around," he said.

Opening my eyes, I am looking right at Jade's knees. They are firm little numbers, suggesting a history in sports—crew at Western, if memory serves correctly. She remains confident enough to let them drop from a mid-thigh robe with Japanese undertones, the Far East via the Bon Marchè. She notices me waking on the couch and smiles down. She is a pretty girl—not a classic beauty who sends a artist scrambling for his paints and canvas, but a true blonde who dolls up real nice for those glossy feather-lit mall shots.

"Morning, Goldilocks," she says. "You look like you got some bad porridge."

I sit up and grin rather than risk talking. I am a victim of gen-X hospitality—a bender at night and a big bowl of cereal for breakfast. Mike is rattling in the kitchen, looking only slightly worse for wear in unlaced high tops, sweats and a Huskies sweatshirt.

"Hey, Casey. Want a bagel?"

"Sure."

"What time is your flight again?" This comes, for God knows what reason, for the hundredth time in two days.

"4:30."

We both eye the clock, a modern affair with numbers simply stuck on the white plaster of the apartment wall.

"No problem," he says.

Jade jerks the blinds open, revealing Seattle's skyline in the distance. The city is up and running. My initial sense of relief at being removed from the hustle is soon replaced by guilt for not being a contributing member—a side effect of being reared in the Yuppie age. I ask Jade how she copes. She smiles and stretches her arms overhead, raising the robe a few dangerous inches. I instinctively look for my bagel.

"I don't usually go in until around noon. It takes thirty minutes off my commute." She also works for her dad's construction company, with its odd work schedule that precludes Mike from tripping north for a dead friend but allowed them both to take a weekday off to entertain me. In an effort to show me how they have come to accept Seattle and visa versa, we left the apartment late yesterday morning, lunched at a small seafood place that "only the locals know about" and boycotted the tourist standards of the Kingdome and Space Needle for coffee shops and eclectic markets. We ended the evening drinking at a trendy bar in the U District listening to a jazz trio who struggled to look as if they could care less. Still, everyone watched with disinterested appreciation. Even Jade, in her plaid skirt and thick sweater, tapped her foot coolly. People will admit to hating many kinds of music, but no one wants it thought that they don't get jazz.

Watching Mike and Jade spread designer cream cheese on their over-sized organic bagels and sip their coffee with Italian surnames, I am happy for them. The two met up north four years ago, when Jade came up for the summer to run shore excursions for Princess Tours and Mike worked the charter boats. Since then they have bounced up and down the coast in a cycle shared by many of our friends. Summers up north to make money, winters down in the Pacific Northwest where they blow the whole bankroll: Lather, rinse, repeat. It at least gives a soul the illusion of movement. Seattle has always been Alaska's sophisticated stepbrother, and everyone has an aunt or uncle down in Kirkland or Puyallup who allows them to stay a while and dip their toes into the Outside.

Now Jade and Mike are attempting to break the cycle. Mike is a site foreman with a new company F-150 and the bulk of Jade's wardrobe now requires dry cleaning. Last night over drinks they decided to purchase the Black Lab puppy they looked at last week, a modern version of commitment. The steady money and the implications the puppy carries—a yard for the dog, a house with the yard, a family for the house—hang around Mike and Jade like a warm comforter on a rainy morning.

"Sorry we couldn't hook up with Kristen last night," Mike says, getting up for more coffee.

"That's cool." I try to continue the nonchalance I overplayed last night upon hearing Kristen couldn't join us for dinner. "We'll get to visit during the flight."

"Her little boy wasn't feeling good," Jade says.

I grin thanks and decline Mike's offer of coffee. This current layer of mental fog may serve me best by hanging around a little longer. We have yet to talk about poor dead Danny, and I now doubt we will.

I excuse myself to take a shower. Their bathroom is a cramped little affair with a definite feminine flair—framed poems, potpourri sprouting everywhere and, most unnerving, a cutesy photo of the happy couple atop the toilet tank. Even true love should know some boundaries. I emerge to find Jade waiting for the bathroom with a bandolier of beauty items and undergarments. She grins.

"Kristen called for you."

"Okay."

Jade sweeps by and wipes herself a clear swath in the steamed mirror. "She's going shopping at Bellevue Square this morning. She's coming by about one to take you to the airport so Mike doesn't have to drive down and back."

She is still smiling about this when she shuts the door. I take a deep breath and walk into the living room, where Mike has surrounded himself on the couch with work drawings and purchase orders for drywall and rebar.

"You got the message about Kristen?"

I nod. "Mind if I call my folks?"

He points to a wall phone in the kitchen and returns to his papers. I dial my parents' number. I hear the ringing and can see the rattling old green monster that has hung in our hallway for twenty years.

My father answers. His tone on the telephone will forever be one of confusion, either for the mechanism itself or as to why anyone is calling him in the first place.

"Pop. It's Casey."

"Hey there," he says. "Are you in Juneau yet?"

I've explained my itinerary to my dad several times this week, but like most Alaskans he doesn't put much faith in travel plans. He knows they are fickle, but remains optimistic.

"No, Seattle still. I get to Juneau tonight. Hopefully I can catch the last LAB flight home. If not, tomorrow morning, I guess."

"Well, it's raining a little today but I think the planes are still flying." I hear my mom pick up the kitchen extension. She is not so intimidated by the phone, but prefers to use it in tandem.

"Hi, honey. Are you in Juneau yet?"

"No, Mom, Seattle. What's new?"

"Oh, not much. They're paving the street behind us today so there's lots of noise. That's going to leave Stinson Street and the road to the channel as the only dirt roads in town. Something, huh?"

"Yeah. What's next, stoplights?"

"Better not be," Dad says. "Any luck on the job search?"

Thanks to their post-Depression upbringing, my folks doubtlessly envision me having spent the last month rising each morning with a new suit and stack of resumes. Best not to bore them with the actual details.

"Not real good," I say.

"I read the other day how there's a recession on down there," Mom says.

"I believe it."

Dad coughs. "Well, there's always work up here."

"And you have a place to stay," Mom adds.

"I know." I try to sound annoyed by the suggestion but it warms me like hot chocolate in a paper cup. "I just don't want to have to start this whole thing over again six months down the road."

I can hear them nodding over the phone.

"We'll talk when I'm get there," I say. "But I just don't know what to do."

My parents sigh together.

"Well, son," Dad says. "I wish I knew what to tell you."

So do I. I want them to tell me where my next job is, how that girl in Denver was wrong to leave, a lot of things. Growing up we are convinced our parents don't know any better than we do, yet it's still a disappointment to discover we were right.

"Well, I better run," I say. "I just wanted to let you know I'm still on schedule. I'll call from Juneau tonight."

"Say hi to Mike for us," Dad says.

"Is he still with that girl?" Mom says.

"Yes, he is."

"I was never really sure about her."

"I'll pass that along," I say. "Love you guys."

"We love you, son."

The world sat crisp and cool outside Marlene's door and crunched under Danny's boots. The clouds and mist tried to pull apart, and the distant mountains even revealed a few honest blue patches. A row of nearby houses hid the docks, but Danny heard someone's diesel chugging away, monopolizing the morning air.

That rust spot near the Chevelle's rear bumper looked a little worse. Damn salt water. Danny picked at a few oxidized flakes and promised himself he would take the ferry into Juneau sometime and hit a body shop. He had used his first boat share to purchase the 1970 Chevelle eight summers ago sight unseen from a guy in Seattle and barged it up. Danny had only asked the Chevelle to look good, score girls and drive fast on the limited roads his hometown offered. The car had accomplished all this and still went strong, like a good range horse with only the occasional stumble in its step.

He swung first by the post office with Marlene's letters and then idled his way through downtown. A few businesses were already pulling plywood from their storefronts in preparation for the coming cruise ship season, but none of the summer restaurants were open yet. Once again, it would be The Galley for coffee. Danny slid the Chevelle in just shy of the eight-table restaurant's picture window, allowing him a view inside at the current patrons and one last chance to dash if he didn't like what he saw.

He got out just as the police Bronco rolled up behind him. The town's lone patrol car needed a good bath if not a complete replacement. Through the dirt-streaked windshield Hallstrom nodded hello in a way indicating more to follow. Danny shut the Chevelle's door and waited.

For the last twelve years Hallstrom had played the double duty of police chief and basketball coach at the high school. Which job caused him more grief varied with the time of year. Sure, rules got bent a little—a kid might get a pass on a speeding ticket if he played well last game, or breaking curfew might earn a player some extra laps—but most in town considered him a stand-up guy and it all worked out in the end.

"Mornin', Danny."

"Hey, Coach."

"You got a little rust starting back here."

Danny nodded. "It happens."

Hallstrom examined the decay, either concerned or considering a citation. "Who you gonna work for this summer?"

Danny saw a few of The Galley's customers glancing out over their coffee cups. "Whoever pays the most, I guess."

Hallstrom agreed with the sense this made. "Sounds about right. I always wondered why you never took up your own boat. You'd have made a decent skipper."

"Never too late," Danny said.

Hallstrom stood tall and this time didn't appear to fully agree.

"Y'know, we try to limit the open gym activities to basketball and use of the weight room. No boxing."

Danny's sore knuckles pulsed. "What'd you hear?"

"Same as I always hear. Enough."

Danny stared right back into The Galley's big window. All eyes returned to their coffee.

"Kid had it coming," Danny said.

Hallstrom exhaled a small cloud. "You could argue we all got something coming, Danny. It just ain't everybody's job to dole it out to each other."

"He can't handle someone posting up on him down low," Danny said. "I'd post and he'd foul me, saying it was his way to keep me from scoring. It finally got to me. Hell, he'd have fouled out inside two minutes in a real game."

"It ain't a real game, Danny. Besides you've got three inches and thirty pounds on the kid. And eight years."

Danny grinned down at the dirt. "I just think if he's gonna be down low he's got to learn to play defense on someone who knows how to post up."

Hallstrom tapped on the Chevelle's trunk. "He's fast enough to play small forward or big guard. That's my plan. We'll see. The kid is good, Danny, there's no denying it. He's in line to have one hell of a senior season." Hallstrom waited for Danny's eyes to meet his own. "He's got your number, y'know."

Danny exercised his sore fingers. "Yeah, I guess I let his cocky attitude get under my skin, but…"

"No, I mean he's taking your number. Thirty-four, your old jersey." He must have noticed Danny's gaze. "C'mon, Danny, it can't just lay around the equipment room forever. It's the only one that fits him and the other guys have their jerseys picked out from last year. And the school can't afford to buy new ones."

Most boys who grew up in town avoided Danny's jersey, fearful they couldn't measure up to its history of game-winning shots and single-season scoring records. Granted, this kid was new to town, but he knew what he was doing.

Hallstrom picked again at the rust.

"The kid says he won't press charges, doesn't want any hassle. Hell, a black eye at sixteen is a badge of honor. His old man ain't so easy but I think I can work on him. But you know we have a hard time finding and keeping superintendents at the school, Danny. Especially the way this guy dragged his family up here mid-year. If people start beating up his kid, he's liable to head back south."

Danny toed the dirt near the Chevelle's rear tire. Hallstrom put a hand on his shoulder and looked to be deciding on a suitable punishment. Jail wasn't warranted. Danny half expected the Coach to just assign him a few wind sprints. Damned if Danny wouldn't have just started into them right there in the street.

"Good enough, then. We'll talk more later." Hallstrom patted Danny's shoulder and headed back to his Bronco. "Watch out for that rust."

All the regulars waited inside The Galley. They all nodded politely when Danny entered. Their eyes said whatever the exchange was outside, they were in his corner.

"Over here, champ." Dustin waved him to an open seat at the counter. As Danny approached Dustin stood and feigned the moves of a boxer, smiling his lopsided smile. Danny returned a few shadow punches, but only body shots. His friend's face was damaged enough, the result of a block and tackle that gave way and smashed his cheek in while working on a gillnetter three years ago. The cheekbone shattered and even after two operations now just sloped lazily down from his left eye to his lip. Since then Dustin always sat as he did today, with his friends to his right and his face resting on his left palm even when he wasn't tired.

"That little shit had it coming," Dustin said. "He can't keep fouling you, even if it was just a pick-up game."

Danny nodded in agreement and ordered some coffee.

"What'd Coach have to say?" Dustin said.

"Just what you would expect," Danny said. "Don't beat up his star players."

Dustin shook his head. "How soon they forget, huh? Hey, you shot out of there pretty quick last night. I tried your place but didn't get an answer."

Danny's coffee arrived and he just sipped it.

Dustin smiled. "The old standby, huh?"

Danny took a little offense, but let the comment pass.

"Where you guys working today?"

"Laying a foundation for that new salmon bake place behind the hotel," Dustin said. "It's a late start but if we finish by June they can still cash in for most of the summer."

Danny nodded in disinterest. Dustin jumped suddenly, revealing his battered left side.

"Hey, check this out. Remember that fat kid, Dick's nephew who came and worked that summer a couple years ago? The lazy sack of shit bookworm?"

Danny remembered. The hefty kid had been studying civil engineering down south and came north to get some "hands on" experience with his uncle's construction outfit. Danny and Dustin had also worked there that summer. The kid was handier with calculators and equations than a hammer and shovel, but he'd come around by September. Still, his die had been cast early by his co-workers and the kid left town just as chunky and melancholy as he arrived.

"Josh," Danny said. "Right?"

"Yeah," Dustin said. "He's dead, dude."

"Dead?"

"Dead. In Africa." Dustin refitted his face to his palm. "I guess he graduated in that engineering crap and got on with some international company building roads. They sent him over to some shit country to build a bridge."

"Africa." Danny wondered if The Galley had a globe.

"So they're working at some site and he just falls," Dustin said. "Falls right down into the valley or canyon or whatever they're building a bridge across. That was that."

"Dead in Africa." Danny recalled Josh being from Idaho or somewhere thereabouts. And he ended up dead halfway around the world. "Jesus Christ. That is just freaky."

"You said it." Dustin started back into his omelet. Danny sat and drank coffee for another half-hour, listening to Dustin and the other customers. They talked about boats and tourists and plans to get the hell out at the end of the summer. They talked politics and about this new Clinton guy running in the fall, how he was for the workingman and how some ex-mistress of his planned on baring her whole package in an upcoming *Penthouse*. Danny just kept thinking about dead Josh. Danny never was particularly fond of the kid and surprised himself by remembering his name. But now he imagined Josh's fleshy carcass laying at the bottom of that jungle valley, surrounded by plants Danny couldn't even dream of, atop a moist earth crawling with bugs as big as his swollen hand.

Danny excused himself at about 11:30, promising to call Dustin later for beers. The clouds had lifted enough to allow a few planes to fly overhead. At least there would be mail today, maybe something interesting. Only TV awaited him at home, and nothing good came on until two, even with the satellite. Danny would take a drive. The town could claim maybe twenty miles of honest road and the Chevelle had been cruising them all for eight years. Danny felt confident the car simply knew the way and could go without him. Today especially he felt just along for the ride.

He drove by the high school parking lot and its assortment of hand-me-down cars. Bobby's Jetta stood out like a sore thumb. His dad was the superintendent and he still drove his own damn car to school. The punk sat somewhere in the building happy as shit, a full summer and his whole senior year still ahead of him. All that while Josh lay dead in Africa, bugs chewing on him. It made Danny want to go back in there and pull Bobby out of Mr. Klavano's room, haul him to the centerline of the new gym and punch him again under those fluorescent lights and 2A Division championship banners.

Danny wondered where in Africa Josh met his demise—it was a big damn continent. He felt suddenly bad for not knowing more about Africa, or about Josh, for that matter. And how deep was the canyon he fell into? Danny envisioned it as terribly deep, allowing time for a complete scream and some reflection on the way down. Maybe Josh saw it all tumbling by, that crazy African landscape and big African sky and said "Well, at least I'm not in Idaho." Danny imagined Josh's parents being oddly proud of their boy's exotic death. If one were going to get gobbled up by a faraway land, Africa was a good one. Maybe the kid had a corn-fed Idaho girl who loved him for his husky bookworm self, and he called out her name as he fell. She didn't hear it back in Idaho, where she sat knitting or doing crosswords and waiting for his daily long-distance call. Maybe Josh found some African princess over there and on the way down he let out some tribal scream she taught him. Maybe he just saw the ground coming and said "I'm dead." Or maybe, Danny hoped, Josh watched all that lush, inviting scenery sail past and went to the bottom thinking it would break his fall.

At the far end of the parking lot sat Hallstrom's empty Bronco. He was probably inside the gym pulling out the old #34 jersey, washing and pressing it for Bobby. That was fine with Danny. Hallstrom and that school didn't owe him a thing and Danny didn't owe them anything either. Not one damn thing.

With Hallstrom tucked safely in the high school, the roads of his hometown belonged only to Danny and his Chevelle. He gunned the big 454, which roared and sent up a respectable roost, and he rumbled off down the channel road.

I sit watching TV with Mike. Jade left for work a half-hour ago, giving me a sorority girl hug and a light peck so as not to mess her lip gloss. With Jade's whirlwind of energy gone, Mike and I are left alone to talk about mutual friends we see in passing, about who lives close by but we never get a chance meet up with, and the utterly weird way time passes. In short, we don't talk about much at all. I am anxious for Kristen's arrival. Not just to see her but also to save Mike and I from the ominous silence waiting to fall down onto us. We hold it up with small talk, anecdotes and "remember the time's," but the lulls grow longer and our banter takes on the tone of a meeting where the day's business is resolved yet the attendees feel the need for chitchat. The silence will drop onto us and leave us to watch afternoon TV and realize we don't know our friends anymore. With Danny gone, neither of us wants to lose another friend just yet.

I go for an easy shot, picking up a framed picture of Mike and Jade.

"So what's the deal? You gonna take the long walk?"

Mike gives me a little shove.

"I don't know, man. We talk about it. Jade wants to get into a house and all." He shakes his head as if the immensity of the whole thing is just now hitting him.

"You guys put in the work," I say. "May as well go for the certificate of participation."

He smiles. "I guess. What about you?"

"I'm sure not gonna marry you."

He slaps my shoulder and I return it. The exchange gives me hope.

"Shut up," he says. "You know what I mean. Are you going to try and get something going with Kristen?"

A good volley. "I haven't seen her in years, and, I don't know…"

He senses my flailing and nods with a slow exhale, the physical equivalent of saying "but anyway."

"So, heading home," he says.

I echo him. "Heading home."

"What's it been, three years?"

"Just about. Since that summer all of us worked on the *Kestrel*."

I can see that summer in Mike's eyes. He fixes them on the grey Seattle skyline outside. I know where his mind is, or at least I think I do. Maybe something does always remain.

"You and Jade ever think about going back up?"

Mike grimaces. "Yeah, we do. I do, mostly. We've just got such a good deal going here with her old man, and the money is good. Maybe a trip up for the Fourth, especially if a bunch of you guys are there. Other than that…"

Now it is my turn to nod absently, letting him trail off. A car door slams in the parking lot below. We have heard several already today, but we both know it is Kristen this time. There is some nervous joking, footfalls on the stairs outside and then Kristen is right there in front of me. Then she is hugging me. She is in my arms and I am in hers with the tightest squeeze she has ever given me save for the night of the championship. I suddenly miss Danny something terrible.

"Look at you," she says. She backs up to take me in and bites her tongue on some platitude like "My how you've grown," even though I am the same size as when I last saw her, perhaps even lighter by a few pounds thanks to my road diet.

"Well, look at you," I say and then I do. She has transitioned to the nineties well. Coming of age in the time of DeLoreans, Culture Club and *Miami Vice* makes a person wary of revisiting their past fascinations. Things held aloft by hairspray and slick marketing don't stand up well in this age of flannel shirts and rampant cynicism. Yet Kristen has done it. Her hair has surrendered to gravity in a graceful shoulder-length earth tone and her clothes are the subdued fatigues of the urban intellectual—Birkenstocks, jeans and a brown sweater. In some ways I wanted her to look like another 80's leftover, and have no more appeal than a pop cassette or tacky piece of clothing leaving me to wonder what the hell I was thinking at the time. I look at her now and know exactly what I was thinking.

We are halfway through a nervous exchange about the coincidence and luck of being on the same flight when she hugs me again. This time she doesn't let go.

"I'm so sorry about Danny."

I shrug as much as her embrace allows. "He was your friend, too. We all feel that way."

She backs up but keeps her hands on my shoulders. She smiles like a parent again. Good Lord, I think. She is someone's parent.

She and Mike volley a round of apologies and excuses. Both are sorry they haven't gotten together despite their proximity, but soon, they promise. Kristen cites the unbeatable double defense of her little boy and recent divorce, which she alludes to as simply "that whole mess." Mike once again goes to the well of this gargantuan Mountlake Terrace development, a project I now view as on scale with the Great Wall. Finally, Kristen looks at me.

"Ready to hit the road?"

I glance at my watch but don't actually read it.

"Yeah, we better roll."

I shake Mike's hand, thank him for the hangover and promise to pass on his condolences. He assures me my Datsun will remain safe in their parking lot until my return. Kristen gives him a hug that I study and decide doesn't equal my earlier one. Mike opens the door and gives us a goodbye nod, and Kristen takes my hand to lead me down the stairs. It is the lightest of grasps and perhaps only maternal instinct. A stiff wind could break it. Regardless of motives, I welcome her hand. We still have to drive to Sea-Tac, jet our way to Juneau and then fly another hour in a six-seat plane, but descending those steps I am already halfway home.

Danny's Chevelle lay in the channel almost two days before being discovered. Even at high tide the car was plainly visible, the rear tires and bumper rising out of the tumultuous waters. Truth be told, no one from town went out that way much anymore. There was just no call for it. People began wondering where Danny was after a day, but not with any real concern. Like many folks in these parts, it was not unheard of that he might just disappear for a short stretch, either into his house or off on a state ferry to Juneau. Sometimes a person just needed to get the hell out and be alone for a while.

An LAB pilot flying low and scud running his way to the airstrip finally spotted the car Thursday morning. Hallstrom arrived when the tide was out, and he slipped in a few bigger tidal pools hiking out to where the Chevelle lay upside down. The right side was crumpled and the roof compressed, all the windows cracked and spider-webbed. Danny lay inside, bloated and drowned several times over by two days worth of tides.

Hallstrom called for the ambulance and fire truck but they were slow in coming. The fire department was a volunteer outfit and the EMT's needed time to leave their various jobs, go get dressed at the fire station and then drive their equipment out the rough channel road.

"No need to hurry," Hallstrom told them over his radio. "Don't beat up your new rig on that damn road."

Water already trickled at the channel's far end when the ambulance and fire truck arrived. Jim Sollen, the senior EMT and town postmaster, joined Hallstrom down in the channel next to the car. Neither door would open and the driver's side window had been kicked out, no doubt in Danny's attempt to escape. Despite the car's crushed roof a good-sized space remained, big enough that Jim Sollen—no beanpole himself—could slide in and ensure Danny was alone in the Chevelle. Hallstrom guessed he could even squeeze through himself if he sucked in his gut. But when they attempted to drag Danny out his frame wouldn't allow it. That ribcage was just too damn big.

"Well, shit." Sollen stood winded after a third attempt. "I don't think he's coming out without some cutters." He eyed the new fire truck, its flashing red lights popping audibly, and then the channel's far end. "And I don't think we've got enough time before she fills in again."

Hallstrom agreed. They would be standing in three feet of water within ten minutes. Danny would spend one more tidal cycle in his car. They tucked him back inside the Chevelle and hiked back up to the road. Hallstrom radioed back into town and had the desk girl start calling the local outfits to see who could get a crane out there the soonest. By now a small crowd of locals stood gathered back behind the emergency equipment. Hallstrom knew he should rope the whole place off as a crime scene or something like that, but he didn't have any of the loud yellow tape with him and figured the channel belonged as much to them as it did to anyone.

So he stood with them all and watched the water rush in and fill the channel. It rocked Danny's Chevelle back and forth in a tender dance. The people speculated how Danny must have gone in at low tide to crush the top like that and then he just couldn't get out. Some insisted Danny was lucky the channel wasn't full of water at the time in that he at least had a chance, while others insisted true luck would have landed him in the channel at high tide. The top wouldn't have been crushed and he probably could have scrambled out. Danny often drove with the windows open, they said, and he was a strong swimmer, even in the cold waters of Southeast. Hallstrom just eyed the Chevelle's waltz and didn't see how luck, good or bad, had anything to do with all of this. Everyone knew Danny and how he drove, and everyone knew that road. From there on it was just inevitable.

Hallstrom heard the tracks of the big Link-Belt grinding down the channel road thirty minutes before the crane actually came into view. It would be dark by the time the channel drained, so he sent a local kid into town to round up some floodlights from the construction site down by the hotel. Late afternoon found people talking about Danny and basketball, how his jersey ought to be retired or something thereabouts. Hallstrom didn't see any way around dedicating next year's season to Danny. By dinnertime the crowd at the shore thinned to required personnel and those too old or gossipy to be missed at the table. Everyone recognized the accident as a damn shame, but something similar had happened before. A long time ago, everyone agreed, though no one could recall a name.

I babble like an idiot as Kristen drives us across the 520 bridge, and soon the buildings of downtown Seattle are peering over our shoulders. I refuse to let the car be overtaken by the silence most recently observed on Mike's couch. I talk about my drive, my drunken visit to Bozeman, anything I can dredge up. I am thankful to be free of any embarrassing maladies—hernia, hemorrhoids, dysentery—for I would have described them in full detail rather than surrender the car to silence.

The car's backseat is a testament to consumerism, full of bags reading like the directory of Bellevue Square Mall. This only endears Kristen to me more. I guess you can take the girl out of the eighties, but…and so on.

"Where's the little guy?" I scan the backseat, half-expecting his head to emerge from a JCPenney bag.

"I divorced him." She follows with a laugh. This is not a new joke for her. "The one I kept is down at my aunt's place near the airport. We have to stop by and get him and my other stuff for the flight."

"I look forward to meeting him," I say and feel suddenly stupid. I imagine myself shaking hands with a two-year old, perhaps inquiring about his baby teeth. And then he craps his pants.

"So how long has it been?" she says, handing me a bomb with too many wires.

"Since…?"

Kristen laughs and gives me a sidelong glance.

"I don't know. Pick one. Since you've been home, since you saw Danny, since you and I have seen each other."

I ponder the order of options and fold.

"I haven't been home for real in about three years. Since

the last summer I worked there. I went up for Christmas a year and a half ago. I guess that's the last time I saw Danny."

"About the same for me," she says. "I went up for my cousin Jenny's graduation last spring, but only for a couple of days. I didn't recognize any of the kids in the high school halls."

I nod, then silence. The Kingdome drifts by, looking older and dirtier than I've ever noticed.

"So what's up with you?" she says. "You're not making rockets anymore?"

"Missiles, actually." I start, but then shake my head. "Nothing now. Layoffs, y'know. There's not as many people to shoot them at, and I was judged to be expendable."

Kristen grimaces. "Weren't you seeing some girl out there, too?"

I laugh at her knack for conversational Achilles' heels.

"She shared the missile-maker's opinion of me."

"I'm sorry." Kristen places a hand on mine.

"No big deal," I say. "Neither was anything I saw as long term." I laugh. "Both had too many destructive undertones."

I don't know exactly what I mean by that, and neither does Kristen, but we share a knowing laugh.

"So what next?" she says.

"I don't know. The job market is pretty bad everywhere, and I guess there's a recession on. I might try here or down in Portland. At least I can choose where I am unemployed."

She nods and guides us off an exit just south of Boeing Field. "Are you going to stay the summer at home?"

"I really don't know."

"Might be good for you," she says, knowing what I want to hear. "There are always jobs. Stay at home, save some money. Make a fresh start come fall."

"Yeah," I say, energized by the thought. Heading south with a fat bankroll just when the September rains hit and the higher peaks start getting snow, stepping off the jet down where it's still summer and conveniences abound.

"I'm thinking about it," she says.

"Really?"

She surrenders a nod. "I need it, Casey. I need the money for one, and Tony says I can give tours for him full-time. Then I figure I can help with the shore-ex stuff for Westours one or two days a week. And I want Jack to see a little of where I grew up, even if he's too small to appreciate it." She stops reluctantly at a red light, sighing like she deserved it. "I need to go home. The Outside has just kicked my butt lately. Between Jack and the divorce, everything is just moving a little too quick right now. I need to recharge my batteries."

I nod absently. My mind is already scanning the crowd at Danny's funeral, searching for any skippers who might need a hand for the summer, perhaps one who can make missiles.

She shrugs. "Yeah, I just don't know."

This from the girl who eight years ago had everything mapped out. She would study marketing at the U of W, work summers on one of the bigger Holland America boats, and then a career as an overseas buyer for Nordstrom, taking her to places that my public school geography left me at a loss to locate. Now, with a transcript boasting only two quarters at the U and three at Highline Community College, driving a Ford Tempo borrowed from her aunt, Kristen strikes me as very brave.

"It'll be weird without Danny," I say.

"Yeah, it will," she says. "Even though, man, I haven't really talked to him in probably four years. I guess I would hardly know him anymore."

Now it is my turn to put a calming hand on hers. I do so only momentarily.

"Yes, you would," I say. "It's been a long time but you would."

"I had a crush on him, you know?" she says. "Not a real big one, just the one I guess all the girls in town were required to have."

I grin through a vague grey happiness that Danny is gone and then a quick flush of guilt. It all passes smoothly, for I am not learning anything new.

"He did have a way about him."

She smiles. "He did. He wasn't the best looking, but he was built kind of big and strong and girls just knew they were supposed to like him."

Danny must have known this, and I always wondered if the ultimate measure of our friendship rested in his never having taken Kristen out to the channel in his Chevelle and pinned her to the backseat. He had been the Southeast Alaska version of a gentleman, and I hope he knew how I appreciated it.

"I had a big crush on you," I say for no reason, and don't qualify mine. It truly went beyond the mere small-town call of duty.

"I know." Her grin says she was counting on this. "And don't you miss that?"

I think of analyzing every word she wrote in my yearbook, of knowing her class schedule better than mine, and of the knot my stomach tied itself in every spring when the college guys showed up in town.

"I guess."

We are driving in a residential area now, all chain-link fences and four-way stops. Jets roll by overhead on final approach for Sea-Tac to the south.

"I mean the whole feeling of a crush," she says. "Nowadays you're just hot for someone or something vague like that. Those crushes were just pure potential. We knew if we actually did something, it would all become real and disappointing. But in that crush stage, I felt removed and safe. I could imagine anything happening."

She stops at the next intersection, allowing a Big Wheel to cross. The rider, maybe seven years old and all business, appears bound to some high-level backyard fort meeting. The birch trees above us, previously calm, shuffle seductively. It gets the attention of both the Big Wheel rider and myself. In the distance I see a Boeing 757 descending beyond the houses and trees to the airport. Kristen starts through the intersection.

"Want to see something cool?" I say.

The smile she gives me is trusting, but not fully.

"Sure, I guess."

"Pull over right here."

She sidles the car up to the curb on the opposite side of the intersection. I get out before she can form the question I know is coming. I scan the skies to the north over Elliot Bay. An Alaska Airlines 737 roars overhead, but I doubt it will be sufficient. My heart warms at the sight of a big fat United 767 lining up a few miles behind the Alaska airplane.

Kristen is out of the car and sees me looking north.

"I hate to tell you this, Casey, but I have seen jet planes before. Several times. You know, we're actually supposed to be on one in a couple of hours."

She smiles and I return it without speaking. I am enjoying the role of man with a mission, though I doubt I am fooling her. I point at the United jet.

"All planes put off a wake, just like a boat," I say. "Except where a boat's just rolls off to the shore, a plane's falls down and trails behind it. It rolls off the wingtips and comes down like a spinning tube of air. Sometimes when it's really raining you can see them hanging off the wingtips like tubes of condensation."

I look to her hopefully, wanting her to have noticed in the past.

"Okay, sure." She laughs. "I see it all the time."

"I'm not kidding." I say, but also laugh. The 767 is almost on top of us now. The Big Wheel rider is parked and watching us, thankful for his youth and sanity. "We studied this in my aerospace classes. Bigger planes like this one create a real strong wake. I saw it in the trees earlier, I think. The winds must be just right to allow them to drop down here."

Kristen takes me on faith and steps up beside me to face the oncoming jet.

"You need to know this to make missiles?"

I shake my head. The big jet is a safe five hundred feet overhead, but I am still near yelling to her. "No. I've actually never seen it for real. I just know it's supposed to happen."

Kristen mouths "okay," but the plane is passing over the top of us. The engine noise steals her voice. We stand and wait. Nothing happens. I cast a glance over my shoulder at the plane, now disappearing beyond the horizon of trees and homes down to the tarmac. Kristen takes my hand firmly and the leaves overhead rustle. We look up to see the trees swaying.

"Oh, yeah," Kristen says and laughs aloud in a way one wouldn't expect from a recently divorced single mother. I tighten my grip on her hand, as if the wingtip vortice might pull her up and away. By the time it drops out of the tree onto us there is barely enough power to kick up the dirt at our feet. She is still laughing, though, especially when an errant leaf perches in her hair just below her left ear. The wind picks up her hair just enough and then lays it back down. The leaf remains, and I want it to stay there indefinitely. A last few chuckles jump through Kristen as she wipes the dust from her shining eyes and instinctively reaches up for the leaf. In the end, though, she lowers her hand and lets the leaf remain right where the wind put it.

RIVETS

Midway through "Sweet Jane" Duane DeMarco decided he was done. A true professional, he finished out the song.

The fat fisherman finally sent him over. Duane assumed him a fisherman or deckhand, as he smelled of a day's take and appeared unstable with dry land underfoot. Maybe the latter resulted from the six Jack & Cokes he downed before strolling across the empty dance floor to where Duane stood with his RSQ Echo Pro 333 electronic backup machine. Once there, the fisherman stooped slightly, bringing his glazed eyes level with the shorter Duane's, and studied the singer across the six inches separating them. Not once during the song's five minutes did the fisherman's eyes completely focus. Even after Duane finished and set his Telecaster in its stand, the fisherman regarded him like a math quiz for which he'd forgotten to study.

A sweating Kokanee awaited Duane at the bar. Steve, the owner of the Waterlogger, grinned from the taps.

"Got yourself a groupie, eh?"

Duane glanced over his shoulder. The fisherman still eyed the resting Telecaster as if the guitar might leap to life and attack him. In a just world it would.

"You need a goddamn stage," Duane said.

Steve laughed and reached under the bar to turn up the jukebox. "My regulars barely make it across a level floor. They don't need a stage tripping them up."

"A stage separates your act," Duane said. "If I'm down on the same level, it's just like someone from the crowd getting up and singing."

Steve grimaced. Architectural changes at the Waterlogger Bar came at a glacial pace.

"I just don't know," he said. "That's where my foosball tables usually go. It'd be a bitch to move them on and off a stage whenever a singer blows through."

Duane drained his beer. Too many customers entering during the last week had eyed him with disappointment and inquired about the foosball tables.

"I can get you a box from the back to stand on," Steve said. "Or maybe a real tall stool."

"Great. I'd look like a damn baby in a high chair."

Steve shrugged. "I see your point, Dale…"

"*Duane.*" Duane made a mental note to check the name written on the chalkboard outside the front door, just above the burger specials. "Besides, I'm done."

Duane tapped his empty on the bar, hoping Steve would send another free one before his resignation set in.

Steve surveyed his crowd. The fisherman had rejoined his crew in a booth, pointing at the guitar as though it had insulted him. A handful of regulars sat spread along the barstools. In the back two loggers played an ulterior game of pool with a girl too young for the bar swaying to a song too soulful for her Canadian hips.

"Yeah, if you want to cut out early, that's cool. Tuesdays are always slow."

"No, man, I mean I'm done." Duane quickly opened his fresh beer and established ownership with a sip. "*Finito.* As in blasting the fuck out of here."

"Ah, don't let one bad night get you down."

Duane harrumphed. Tonight was no precedent. Duane Demarco was thirty-five and could sing and play just about any song a fishing or logging bar crowd might request. He wore an imitation silk shirt that shimmered in bar lights and hid his extra twenty pounds. His hair hung a little longer than most his age dared, and he covered it with a cowboy hat of sorts that didn't suggest any knowledge of ranching or cattle. He recognized the hat as a fashion risk, but knew male pattern baldness to be a bigger one. In short, Duane DeMarco was old enough to know better.

"How long does it take to get to Seattle from here?"

Steve eyed the ceiling thoughtfully. "Flying?"

"On what you're paying?"

Steve scratched his temple. "Catch a bus down to Victoria, maybe ten hours. Then you could take the Clipper across, another couple hours. That'd be the cheapest and easiest, what with your guitar and little machine there."

Steve was taking this too well.

"I mean it," Duane said. "I don't care about the week left on our agreement."

"That's okay. Help me move the foosball tables up from the back and we'll call it even."

"I'm not kidding, Steve," Duane said. "My brother works for Boeing. He can get me on there. Twenty bucks an hour driving rivets, making airplanes. Full benefits and everything."

"A man your age has to consider such things."

Duane didn't even want to finish the bastard's beer, but did anyway and stood.

"I'm going outside. I'll be back in a little while."

"We'll take care of those tables then." Steve took up a stray rag without thought—not for any particular reason, just as a default bartender action. "I'll watch your stuff."

Duane didn't look back. "Fuck it. Let it get stolen."

"Smart move. Less to carry on the bus."

Outside it was warm for May in British Columbia, and the air on the water hung in a half-assed noncommittal fog. The Waterlogger sat right off the docks, abutting Port Hardy's small downtown. Duane stepped to the railing, lit a smoke, and stared in a direction he hoped to be south. Seattle sat out there roughly twelve hours away, depending on boat and bus schedules. An honest day's travel to his mom's place in Green Lake and Dick's hamburgers and a Starbucks every other block.

His second cigarette found Duane wondering if his Squire Telecaster would float. The Echo Pro machine sure as hell wouldn't, though with its weight and bulky stand he might need Steve's help hoisting the multi-talented monster over the rail. Like the countless unreliable band members Duane bought the Echo Pro to replace, he could easily see himself tossing it into the murky harbor. The machine would doubtlessly continue chiming heartless but technically-perfect versions of "Born on the Bayou" and "Brown Eyed Girl" all the way down.

The guitar, though, boasted a solid alder body and

maple neck. Unless science had changed in the last twenty years, wood floated. All the electronics and hardware might drag the guitar under, but Duane wanted a guarantee. He wanted the Tele to break the black surface with a cliff diver's ripple and plant its fretted neck deep in the muck and mud of the harbor's floor. Mostly, Duane didn't want the guitar coming back.

Duane's mom and brother had gone in together to get him a beautiful Martin acoustic for Christmas six years ago. He'd taken the Martin with him to Ketchikan the next summer, where he canned salmon during the day and wrote songs at night in his little apartment up the hill. That July Duane convinced the Marine Bar to give him a night all to himself. Just a microphone, his guitar and his songs, camouflaged among a few tasteful and reverent covers—John Prine, Lightfoot and the like. The din of college kids, fishermen and cruise ship drunks filled the cramped bar and quickly overpowered his simple little songs like a chunky schoolyard bully. Customers only approached him to request whatever he might know by Jewel, Dave Matthews or Ani DiFranco. It scared Duane to the core how easily his songs bent, folded and disappeared beneath the workings of a standard bar with a substandard crowd. He drank himself shitty on the free beers afforded to performers and stormed out into a Ketchikan summer night's rain. Clutching the Martin by its neck, he walked across the street and tossed the guitar unceremoniously into the cold waters.

He awoke the next morning unregretful. He sold his hardcase at the downtown pawnshop for a quick thirty dollars and spent his day at work dreaming of a southbound Alaska Airlines ticket and twenty dollars an hour punching rivets.

Three days later he answered a knock at his door and found a scruffy man in a Taquan Air jacket holding the Martin.

"This belong to you?" The pilot spoke as if he'd found the guitar rooting around his flower garden.

Duane regarded the guitar with distrust.

"I guess."

The pilot held it out. "I found it down by Metlakatla. Our dispatcher said it might be yours."

Duane took the guitar in and set it carefully in a corner, wary to touch much less play it. One didn't just pick up a resurrected guitar and start strumming.

The next night he decided the guitar's return was a sign to press on. What better way to write the songs that needed to be written about this region than with a guitar soaked in her waters? He wanted the Martin to hum with the depth of the surrounding mist, to cry like the slap of a weeklong rain on flat water, to resonate like a thousand drunken stories told in bars until they became true. Duane wanted the guitar to moan like the boards of the boats she had shared those Southeast waterways with for three days.

The guitar sounded like shit. The salt water had thrown her five fathoms out of tune, the tuning heads moved with a chunky grind, and some sort of odiferous algae had made a home in the far corners of the sound box. Duane bought his hardcase back from the pawnshop for forty dollars and took the Martin south at the end of the season. He hid it deep in his mother's basement, though in recent phone calls she complained of a smell when she did laundry. Duane doubted the Martin would be waiting when he got home this time.

The riveter job at Boeing had been mentioned eight years ago at a family dinner. Duane's engineer brother brought it up just that once, most likely at their mom's urging. He hadn't broached the subject since. Still, Duane simply assumed the job would always be there, hanging just over his shoulder like a ripcord.

Driving rivets, putting airplanes together piece by piece—that was real honest work. A guy could take comfort in such authenticity while gridlocked on I-5 with the suit & tie SUV set bound to and from their sterile fattening pens. It was loud and obtrusive work, the kind that might take a finger or at least leave a nasty bruise if Duane wasn't careful. After work he could sit in a neighborhood bar drinking Coors Light and bitch about the union. Duane would pack his own thick homemade sandwiches for lunch, or on nice days buy something greasy and hot from the lunch truck in the parking lot. He could eat sitting outside with coworkers, watching the jets they put together roar out over Puget Sound from Sea-Tac off to places they never cared to go. The job would roll on all year and through all the seasons, not ending until Duane decided to stop or the world ran out of rivets. He could still play guitar at home and maybe at a club one or two night a week, but would tell no one at work. Still, they would somehow hear about how that DeMarco guy down on the assembly line played guitar and sang. He would wave off any inquiries with responses equal parts humility and suggestion. *Oh, I used to play*, or *Yeah, I tried making a go of it*. He would downplay his talent repeatedly, until one Friday night the whole work crowd ended up drinking in some bar with a band playing and Duane would be forced to the stage. The tired front man would welcome the break and turn over his mike and guitar. Duane imagined a sincere axe like a worn Les Paul Gold Top. Duane would humbly lead them through a couple classic 1-4-5 numbers, a few reliable bar covers, and finally some solo originals. His coworkers would be amazed and pass on their newfound respect and admiration come Monday morning. Most importantly they would sit there that night and listen to his voice and his hands on that Les Paul and they would goddamn love it.

Settling Outside would take some adjusting, for sure. A decade now lay between Duane and his last year-round job, trying to sell neon BC Rich guitars to high school kids at a small guitar shop in Bothell. At the time he played with a bunch of guys from school who Duane thought understood what he wanted to say. Then that damn Cobain and his hamfisted shoe-gazing buddies hit the scene and those bastards traded in integrity for distortion pedals and feigned angst. One spring the guitar shop's owner copped to snorting all the store's profits up his nose and was forced to sell the shop to some new dot com millionaires who turned it into a coffeehouse. Betrayed on all fronts, Duane had come north to work the canneries for some quick cash and a fresh start in the fall.

Ten winters later, Duane now recognized himself in the unmistakable grip of seasonal drift. And for good reason—optimism came so much easier in six-month increments. If the songs Duane spent the winter writing fell flat with unappreciative Seattleites, maybe the folks up north would dig them. When a good rhythm section failed to materialize during a summer in Skagway or Sitka, he fell asleep each night envisioning a top-notch bassist and drummer just waiting for him to step off the plane in Seattle. Duane went into each summer and winter thinking this would be the time when everything came together. By the time he realized nothing was going to happen, he was halfway through the season. In just a few months he would get a chance to start over again. It took a special type of person and a lot of energy to find hope in both gaining and losing daylight.

Still, some of his best times had come up here. Like the time he hooked up with that bar band in Juneau for jam nights a couple summers back. It had been mainly 12-bar standards, but he had those summertime college kids out jumping much later than they should have been on a work night. Or that little hippie girl in Skagway who waltzed in during his acoustic set at the Red Onion and asked if he knew "Return of the Grievous Angel." He said he did, and damned if she didn't nail every one of Emmylou's harmonies over his attempt at Gram's parts. That drunken crowd even clapped like they had an inkling of the gift they'd received that night. When the song ended he thought he might follow that girl anywhere. She simply said "Thank you" and walked back out the door. He never saw her again, but on the occasions he drank too much he readily admitted he searched every crowd he'd played to since for her eyes.

Then came the nights like this. In the early days these periods of disillusionment coursed through him in an afternoon, passing like a spiritual heartburn. After fifteen years of singing someone else's song to people who weren't listening, these times now hung in longer and made Duane wonder if some permanent damage hadn't been done to his spirit's digestive tract.

He considered a walk up the street to the Mermaid Club, but that hag Carla was probably on stage. The club offered a more base entertainment than the Waterlogger, though not as base as the name implied. A suggestive pole rose from the center of the club's bona fide stage, and the management brought girls like Carla up from Vancouver to dance around it for the fishermen or loggers in Port Hardy for a few days. That was all—just dancing. The club's owner didn't want to wrestle with whatever paperwork nightmare a legitimate strip club required, and after weeks in the woods or on the water, the club's patrons were satisfied watching fully clothed women orbit the pole. Each girl brought an item from their closet at home that struck them as sexy—an evening gown, a schoolgirl uniform, or in Carla's case, an ill-fitting sea-foam green prom dress. Even on the sultriest of nights, the girls left the stage just as clad as they arrived. Carla sometimes removed her glasses for a hint of burlesque, but put them back on for the fast songs as her myopia, combined with the low light, disrupted her balance.

Duane took a shine to Carla when they both arrived in Port Hardy two weeks ago. He assured her his short stint at the Waterlogger was just the beginning of a summer tour of Coastal B.C. and Southeast Alaska. Nothing solid, but he had leads everywhere a fishing boat could tie up and beer was served. Carla had found the strip clubs of Vancouver too cliquey and selective, and planned to use her summer's take from the Mermaid Club to study psychology at Simon Fraser or attend court stenographer school. Both being imported talent, they were housed in the fragrant waterfront hotel across from the Mermaid. Duane courted Carla with a lazy irregularity no judge could consider harassment. He took notice when her room light was on, staged an occasional rendezvous around the snack machines, and went to watch her not-strip on slow nights. She finally came to listen to him a few nights back, though she mostly talked to the bartender and played Tragically Hip and 54-40 songs on the jukebox between his sets. She hadn't even noticed how Duane looked at her while singing "Angel From Montgomery."

He had cornered her the next morning in the hotel café. Canadian through and through, Carla was not prone to missing breakfast, an indulgence that would soon show in her prom dress and tip jar. He pressed for her opinion of his show, but what he got came like reflections of a road trip she had mostly slept through.

"That machine kinda throws me off," she finally said. "Makes all the songs sound real similar."

"I plan on putting a decent band together when I can find one," he said. "But the machine's gonna have to do for now."

She shrugged and pasted more ketchup on her eggs.

"Well, what do they say—don't quit your day job?"

Duane made a snide comment about both his lack of a day job and her powers of perception. He closed with an observation about seeking advice from a stripper who didn't take her clothes off.

She just smiled.

"Well, we're both in this shithole. So I guess you're a singer like I'm a stripper."

Duane grinned and said "Touché." He was unsure if he used the word correctly, but at his age and current lot in life, further opportunities to say it might be limited. He dropped more than enough for both breakfasts on the table, doffed his phony cowboy hat and left. He hoped there was enough change left for Carla to buy some doughnuts and keep eating and getting fatter. Maybe the strain would finally overwhelm that sea-foam green prom dress and her goods would at long last come flopping out for all the fishermen and loggers to see.

When the harbor mist became rain, Duane stayed and smoked. For all its poseur appearances, the cowboy hat provided surprising coverage. He heard footfalls on the boardwalk behind him, but didn't turn around. They sounded jovial and already drunk. Duane didn't need to face more disappointed foosball players.

The footsteps stopped.

"Hey."

Duane turned to find a standard coastal trio—two thick guys in clothes they'd worked in all day if not all week, and between them a tough-looking girl who obviously knew the inverse relationship between latitude and beauty. She appeared to be with the shorter one, but it was still late spring and she didn't look ready to commit yet with summer coming.

"Hey, fella," the tall one said. "You're getting wet."

Duane killed his cigarette on the wet railing.

"I guess so."

"You're the singer here, no?" He pointed at the chalkboard sign near the door. "Dale DeMarco?"

Close enough. "Yeah, that's me."

The tall one patted both his friends' shoulders, letting his bony hand linger a little too long on the girl's.

"I told these two we had to come listen tonight. Y'know that one you sang a couple nights back about weed and whites and wine?"

Duane nodded. "The Lowell George tune."

"Yeah," he said. "You haven't played it yet tonight, have you?"

"No. No I haven't."

The girl released a shiver that ran right up the tall one's arm. The smaller man noticed.

"Okay then." The tall man opened the door. "We'll just be waiting for when you get sense enough to come inside."

"Shouldn't be long," Duane said.

The open door released a blaring shot of a Stones song which the closing muffled a few seconds later. Duane turned back to the direction he hoped was south, but he couldn't see much of anything, much less imagine Seattle out there. The rain came harder now. It plopped and hissed on the flat harbor like Duane thought rivets might, if dropped from far above. The rivets of rain smacked the water, barely stopping at the surface before racing to the muddy floor. Down there they collected with beer bottles and overboard deck equipment, and maybe soon an Echo Pro backup machine and a Baltic Blue Squire Telecaster. When he thought about all her honest alder and maple, he guessed the guitar might float. Then, without even a glance back to where the Telecaster waited for him inside, he knew damn well she would.

ARCHENEMY

I am, for the most part, unremarkable. I am twenty-six years old, a conservative thirty pounds overweight, and I work as a clerk for a well-known chain store offering copying, printing and binding services. The company prefers "copy artist," but in the interest of honest self-appraisal, I decline the title. I hail from Beaverton, Oregon, a collection of Olive Gardens, Red Robins and Pier One outlet stores interchangeable with countless other parasitic suburbs riding the coattails of better-known cities. Combine this heritage with a 2.7 undergrad GPA and half a master's degree from a state university and my milquetoast normalcy solidifies. I have something, though, that sets me apart from most people, an ace up my sleeve. I have an archenemy. Anyone would agree that this is not normal.

Plenty of people dislike, despise or flat-out hate some other person. They can't stand how someone talks or acts or chews with their mouth open. These are not archenemies. I am even wary to say I hate my archenemy, for he is so much more than just a person in the next cubicle who makes endless personal calls while listening to the soft-rock station playing the hits of the 80's, 90's and today. You may even be able to initially tolerate a true archenemy, perhaps exchanging respectful witty banter with them like in the movies. But where annoying people are sufferable indefinitely, an archenemy cannot be put up with forever. It is a matter of principles. An archenemy is diametrically opposed to what you stand for, and negates you in the grand tally of souls. Until one of you is defeated, the other's worth is nullified.

I admit this is not the healthiest existence, but I am hardly alone. Look at PETA, religious fundamentalists who blow up abortion clinics, and those Greenpeace kooks who constantly strap themselves to ice breakers and trees. They fling their venomous energy around the globe towards people they've never even met. Where their enterprise is endless and all consuming, mine is focused. In addition, a personalized effort takes less energy and, with some basic time management skills, an arguably normal existence is possible.

My nemesis and I share a number of things in common, an ironic requirement of good archenemies. On the most basic level, we share the Hawthorne district in Portland and the number 14 bus which traverses this slacker-chic area each morning and evening. He enters the bus with no words for the driver and a disinterested scowl for his fellow riders. His look would have you believe he rides by choice—saving the planet and such—but I am confident his patronage of Tri-Met, like mine, is financially imposed. He takes a seat alone or stands and reads his beaten paperbacks—nothing any of the other riders would recognize—or writes in his elaborate notebook. He acknowledges no one, not even me. Some would argue he isn't a proper archenemy if he doesn't even recognize me. I contend he is so wrapped up in himself he won't know he has an archenemy until it is too late.

I'm sure he would claim age is meaningless, but I guess him to be in his mid-thirties. He is already free of hair, though a simple "bald" seems too docile a description. He takes great pleasure in the surprising planes and angles of his shaved head and parades as if he willed his own hairlessness. He is belligerently bald. His dress is unmistakably urban, carefully disheveled and dancing a fine line between retro-kitsch and Goodwill crap. His only Northwest influences are a pair of black thick-soled shoes for the rainy season and a stiff navy Dickies jacket meant to show some commonality with the blue-collar man.

His jumping-on point is a few influential blocks downstream from mine, near my sterile apartment conveniently located across from a Safeway and Blockbuster. This allows me to be safely seated near a window when he boards. He lives in a stylishly worn apartment building across from a cheapy theatre whose marquee boasts only art films and marathons of previously banned cartoons. His building is peopled by standard urban rebels occupying the lowest trenches in the war against conformity—clerks employed by porn shops, comic book vendors and used record stores specializing in vinyl, and the black-clad clumps of judgmental grad students who buy back my used books at Powell's downtown. These are his henchmen.

His apartment must be the center of the building's activities, as any archenemy's hidden fortress should. Perhaps *fortress* is too strong for what I envision—a living room of beaten furniture and clutter he hopes guests will take as bohemian, walls covered with tastefully-offensive art and posters boasting underground bands from ten years ago that no one has ever heard of, proving he was there first. There are racks of real records and a surprisingly clean kitchen capable of whipping up only foreign food, perhaps a recipe he picked up while Eurailing across Italy or in the Orient hunting the ultimate Thai stick.

All this is, of course, conjecture. I have never been inside his apartment and doubt I will be until the day I am kidnapped and tortured there in a showy but easily escapable fashion. He is my nemesis and such behavior is expected. In my inevitable escape I will destroy his entire lair—not out of spite or a lust for destruction, but simply as my duty. I will somehow ignite an ancillary fire, turning to ashes the Bukowski books and Henry Rollins spoken word videos I know are there, melting and bubbling his Laurie Anderson LPs and his autographed copy of Lou Reed's *Metal Machine Music*. I hope to accomplish all this without damaging any of his neighbors' apartment or belongings. Annoying and pretentious as they are, my battle is not with them and they may have pets. Exactly how all this will happen is still up in the air, as I don't yet know the apartment's layout.

Our second commonality is an inconspicuous East Portland intersection that plays home to my copy store, an AMPM mini mart, and kitty-corner near the bus stop the Java House, where my archenemy works as a waiter. I regularly volunteer to make the short coffee run for all the copy artists. The Java House is everything you'd expect from a locally-owned Northwest coffeehouse. NPR plays on the radio, amateur art covers the walls, coffee names ring with exotic literary undertones, and the servers—my archenemy especially—treat the customers with the minimum courtesy required by law. Still, their cheesecake danish cannot be denied and the atmosphere is refreshing after days spent among bright walls, big windows and posters advertising even more vivid color reproductions. Waiting for my order, I scan the rack containing *The Willamette Week*, *The Portland Mercury* and other subversive urban literature. I also study my archenemy. He sees me regularly but never acknowledges me, and I plan to use this anonymity to my full advantage. Reconnaissance is easier when one can move unwatched, and knowledge, they say, is half of the battle.

If I appear to have a handle on the whole archenemy thing, this is because my coffeehouse adversary isn't my first. Like most, I grew up with schoolyard bullies and hallway snobs, but my first and only other archenemy appeared my first week into a graduate writing program at the state university just a few hours south of Portland. Dr. Michael Talvakas—MFA from Iowa, PhD in Rhetoric, published several times over in *The Atlantic Monthly* and *The Paris Review*, and director of the writing program. He was author of a little-known but critically-lauded collection of short stories and working on a novel Knopf was itching to publish once he got time to properly finish. Between him and that free time sat a group of fresh college grads who hoped two years under his tutelage would enable us to tell the stories we didn't think we could at the time. We were there to be writers and he was there to save future editors time by heading our mediocre efforts off at the pass. He said as much the first day of class, lording from his podium. Chin up and wearing classic collegiate fatigues, elbow pads and all, he looked like he'd mugged Ward Cleaver on his way across campus. His clothes and hair were purposefully rumpled, an attempt to appear the frumpy genius. He told of his struggle for publication and listed his own collection, *Her River and Other Aberrations*, as required reading.

Although even the smallest student could've easily taken him in a street brawl, we cowered from Talvakas and his 143-page book of cynical erudite drunks who slept around and then quoted Proust and Rilke to each other in the afterglow. We wrote and wrote and got together to discuss our collective hatred of him, all the while individually plotting how to win his praise before the others. We huddled over our microbrews and greasy nachos at the college bars like we envisioned Faulkner and Hemingway doing in 1920's Paris. We wanted to satisfy him and to my knowledge never did. Talvakas dismissed everything we submitted as derivative and unattached. The rare praise he gave went to the work and not the writer, as if the story was a last second shot hucked from half court and sent through the hoop by luck alone. My own work was too pedestrian, too distant from its settings and characters, which in the end he didn't even care to get closer to—his actual margin notes. I fumbled through the year, clinging to C+'s like monkey bars too far apart.

Summer finally arrived and I took a projectionist job at a Portland Regal Cinemas near Lloyd Center. I held the belief that storytelling was storytelling, be it cinematic or written, and much could be learned watching through my small portal above those half-empty multiplexes. Though I failed to glean much—*Mission Impossible 2* and *Big Momma's House* dominated the summer screens—I managed to stay cool as one could in a polyester vest and with the help of free buttered popcorn began adding my present extra thirty pounds. Out from Talvakas's intimidating shadow, I formulated plans to bring about his downfall. Nothing violent or illegal, just something to send him crashing to Earth in front of my grad school cohorts. As a last resort, I decided to pen a fine story he couldn't deny. Every day I watched and reflected on my every activity, waiting for this real story to reveal itself. As both summer and my imagination waned, Talvakas's image loomed larger. I expected to see him towering Godzilla-like over campus come September.

I couldn't have been more surprised when, in late August, he strode into my Regal Cinemas. I was on break, visiting a friend working the ticket booth, when Talvakas bought four tickets to *Dinosaur* and breezed off towards the concessions stand without even a glance my way. Two standardized children and a severe woman in ill-fitting cargo shorts and Birkenstocks joined him a few minutes later. Her hair bun screamed with the tension of suspension bridge cables. No sooner did Talvakas receive his popcorn then the woman, apparently Mrs. Talvakas, eyed his four tickets with disgust and dragged the whole lot to the ticket window. She demanded an exchange for four tickets to *Chicken Run*, which my friend informed her was sold out until late that night. The tirade she unloosed on her husband had every Regal Cinemas employee quaking in their polyester and shook crows from trees as far as Hood River. She let him have it and he took it all quietly. From the back of the booth, I had to grin.

Talvakas's next look confirmed he recognized me. He would remember recognizing me and he would remember my grin. It told me not to bother returning to his classroom that fall—a good thing, considering my grades and the bank balance my Regal Cinemas pay had left me. I wasn't worried, and now had no reason to return. Michael Talvakas had been defeated.

The final element my archenemy and I share, and the linchpin of our polarity, is words. We are both writers, or at least purport to be. Every Monday his coffeehouse holds an open mike night I occasionally attend but only to listen. He isn't the host, leaving that responsibility to a thick girl with t-shirts and hair of competing raven blackness, but he is a force. He is an urban street poet. Granted, I've never heard him use the term, but his persona and prose scream it. First and foremost he is from New York, or simply "The City" in his writing, where it pops up with the annoying regularity of junior high erections. Countless times I've overheard—not eavesdropped on, mind you, just overheard—him deriding Portland's urban landscape, nothing compared to "The City." These Portlanders eat it up, traitorously agreeing with the shortcomings of their blue-collar river queen. What events separated him from his home I don't know, but I think he more enjoys being from there than actually *being* there. If a lion allows himself to be caught and put in a faraway zoo, one can only assume he wasn't the most able lion in that jungle.

He spends the better part of the night pacing, making overt last-minute scrawlings in his notepad, sighing loudly when the big girls and waifish boys read their "dear diary" poems of dueling self-love and self-loathing. He puts himself late on the list, knowing how the opening act/headliner mechanism works. After a last minute smoke and glare at the street—perhaps towards my well-lit copy and print center—he enters and takes a chair where others stand and pulls the microphone down. Opening his notebook, he takes us into his city. The sun rarely shines there but when it does it rises over slate grey skies—if any writer ever comes up with a grey sky that isn't *slate* grey, please award him or her the Pulitzer without question. His city is locked in those desperate hours when no one goes to work or loves truly or even eats a decent meal. The city's inhabitants talk only about lust and hate and religious flaccidity and life's contradictory nature. His tone and attitude are obvious—not a person in that coffeehouse, much less in Oregon, maybe even west of Ohio, could survive inside one of his poems.

One could argue I am jealous. Maybe of his city, since my own birthplace falls so short of his. I am wary to even say I'm *from* Beaverton, as any place made up of so many apartment complexes and glass-faced business centers seems incapable of producing actual people. Rather these suburbs are filing cabinets for lives awaiting stapling, collating and copying. My adoptive home of Portland is equally elusive, a well-intentioned schizophrenic peopled with executives bicycling downtown bridges in zip-away pants and concrete hippies strolling Burnside with laptops and cellphones in hemp satchels.

Could I be jealous that he is actually writing? Albeit pretentious, he is creating. In two years I haven't written anything other than a stern note to a co-worker who failed to properly clean the break room microwave—to my credit the note was concise and sharp and the microwave remains spotless. My archenemy lives like an artist. Even his time at work, with the Java House's snooty paperback exchange and countless smokers staring starkly at blank pages waiting for someone to ask what they're working on, exposes him to culture daily. His neighbors no doubt regularly knock on his fortress door hoping to talk books and hear about his latest work. He acts like a writer, which one assumes would increase his chances of success ten-fold. Still, I don't buy it.

A wise man once told me writing and art should be a byproduct of life and not its focus. A life lived fully will yield the stories, then you simply have to skim them from the surface. Okay, no one actually told me that. I made it up myself after running out of money for grad school, but perhaps this explains my creative drought. I can't skim much from eight hours of copying resumes, business proposals, PTA meeting minutes, and a surprising amount of missing pet posters, with an hour for lunch at Quiznos or Pizza Schmizza. The only glimmers of inspiration come from other aspiring writers who bring in short stories or manuscripts to copy. Yes, I read them. Don't be shocked or say "how inappropriate," as if I am violating some sacred trust. They aren't visiting a priest, just getting copies for seven cents apiece. Besides, I don't steal anything. My only encouragement comes from how mediocre most of them are. I know I can do better. My spirits are lifted by the weakness of their work, counting on life's big bell curve. I realize this model of hope won't put me in league with Vince Lombardi, but when you spend all day in an apron with a nametag, you find inspiration where you can.

Mine is not the worst job around, and I've been assured if I apply myself I might someday command a squadron of black-and-white and color copiers and a cluster of aproned drones to control them. Still I must leave someday, though I fear not soon. I have a Visa to pay off and I need a car. Not many new lives are successfully launched on buses or light rail, no matter how many free transfers. Hitchhiking, romantic and safe in Kerouac's time, is now simply a quick way of getting cut to pieces and left in a musty sleeping bag behind a rural Safeway. I don't think tramp steamers exist anymore—no more tramps either, now *homeless*—and too many Doritos and Big Gulps have left me too slow to catch today's fast freights as a hobo—now *transient*. So I will take to the open road when finances allow. I plan to pay for the car full out, owing no one, pull off the lot and drive to the copy store to respectfully rescind my smock with no hard feelings. They've been good with the medical and dental and all. Then I'll cross the street to the Java House and pop my archenemy in the nose. Just a quick one, the kind people receive and in their hearts know they deserved. After that a quick stop at the DMV for fresh plates. This admittedly doesn't keep with my romantic flight, but the whole nose popping seems vaguely illegal and best suited for harder-to-track dealer plates. Still, a run from the law might speed my travel. I tire easily and would be compelled to drive a few hours more each day with Johnny Law in trail.

These loose ends tied up I would be off and driving north. Life sounds real up there, up the Alaska Highway to all the places it goes—Fairbanks, Anchorage, Whitehorse, Dawson. This list is not in proper geographic order, but I plan on buying a good atlas before leaving. Wherever they are, these towns are real places. There is work to be done there, dangerous work that I plan to start respectfully, learning steadily as I go. I will always have a paperback book and pen and paper wherever I go, be it on a boat, a dock, or a dirt road. My rough-and-tumble coworkers will jibe me, but soon develop an odd respect and be pleasantly surprised when, after I am published, they appear subtly in my work. I will work here and there, and will eventually find Karen.

I met Karen my senior year of college. She hailed from Alaska and shared with me a basic philosophy class required for both of us to graduate. She wasn't classically beautiful but bore a rugged sturdy strength, like a Ford F-150 with a good Warn winch. She'd try her best to keep you out of trouble, but if you got into a jam she could pull you out slow and steady. She was still shaped like a woman, despite a deep chest laugh and shoulders suggesting she could press me overhead—maybe not now with my extra thirty pounds. Still, I fell for her. I fell because she laughed that deep laugh when I whispered jokes in class. I fell because of the stories she told of the cold and bears and isolation and wild characters when we would meet to study at the sandwich shop across from campus. Mostly I fell for her because I knew no one else would. That isn't meant as a slight against Karen, maybe just against the people who wouldn't fall for her. Still, I never kissed her, never held her strong hand, never did anything. I always figured I could do all that tomorrow or next week.

I last saw her on campus two days after graduation. She walked with her mousy roommate and smiled upon seeing me. She was going home, flying out of Portland that evening. She would work the summer at home and after that who knew? The way she said that—*who knows?*—made me want to grab her and kiss her right there. Something about the low moody Oregon overcast and the mousy roommate looking on stopped me. The kiss would come across stupid at best, downright creepy at worst. I bid her goodbye and said maybe I'd come up and see her sometime. She said she'd like that and walked away.

That "who knows?" may have landed her anywhere in the last four years, but something tells me she never strayed too far from her native Homer. I may stop there first or maybe last—like I said, I need an atlas—but I will find her. I will find her and concoct some tale about drifting north on my own, but she will know she was my compass. We will fall into a love not indigenous to the lower 48 and the provinces east of Alberta. We will move around the state, working, writing, and living. When I finally publish and return to Portland as the prodigal son to read upstairs at Powell's City of Books, my archenemy will be in the attendance. He won't dare talk of the pop to the nose, and after the crowd thins will ask me to sign his copy and maybe grab a beer. I will graciously refuse the offer—it being late and all—but will sign his book and share a smile with Karen. He will know what I knew with that punch to his nose so much earlier. He has been defeated.

The first Friday evening in October brings serious rain and finds me retreated to the Java House, waiting for the bus. I usually wait at my own workplace, but anger has driven me to the lair of my archenemy for their cheapest cup of plain coffee. Due to temporary budget constraints, all copy artists will be limited to thirty hours per week maximum starting immediately. Apparently management overestimated the printing, collating and stapling needs of the Portland public. I will survive, but my Visa bill will not appreciate this and my used car just rolled forward a few months. I am trapped a little longer—trapped in an apron among the copy machines, trapped on the number 14 bus, trapped kitty-corner from my nemesis.

I sip the bitter coffee, listen to my Discman, and glare at the pages of the latest *Willamette Week*. I am not really reading, just staring hard and hot, and wouldn't be surprised if the pages caught fire. Cars sizzle by outside in Hawthorne's standing water and Miles Davis plays lightly over the coffee shop's radio.

"The Strokes?"

I look up to see my archenemy, arms crossed.

"Excuse me?"

He points at the CD case near my Discman. We have never communicated outside of orders for coffee or copies, and this contact unsettles my footing.

"Yeah," I say. "I like them."

I like them? I must stop talking and get my bearings.

"Fair enough." He pulls his Dickies coat from a nearby rack and slips it on, indicating he is off duty and any server-customer politeness is no longer required. "You should go down to the used music store and buy some Stooges or MC5 records. You'll see who the Strokes wish they were."

And he is out the door. He will beat me to the bus and get a better seat, or at least the pole of his choice to lean on. What did he mean by *used music store*, insinuating the financial situation of a coffee server is so much greater than a copy artist with full medical and dental? And now my music, like my writing under Talvakas, is dismissed as derivative. I have no time to contemplate. The familiar glow of my bus is approaching and I must dash out in the rain.

Tonight's load is unusually light, with seats for both my archenemy and myself. He sits up front near the door, while

I retire back over the rumbling wheel well. He makes no eye contact and stays buried in a thick trade paperback. I eye him occasionally and can't find interest to reopen my *Willamette Week* or listen to my CD player. I just look out the fogged window as the adult arcades and barred grocery stores of East Portland roll by. Winter is no time to have an archenemy. With the rain, wind and reduced daylight, a person's animosity already gets spread too thin. Add in reduced hours and a smaller paycheck, and you just can't give an archenemy proper attention.

We huff and wheeze to a stop at a red light. The intersection sits against an empty lot housing nothing but streetlights and parking spots. People park their used cars in an attempt at the ultimate soft sell. No salesmen or banners, just a FOR SALE sign in the window with an offering price and a number to call. The only other adornments are tickets under the wipers, making the owners aware of their illegal parking. As a result cars disappear for short periods and then return. I usually shop casually each morning, scanning the prices written on the windshields when the bus stops at the light. Tonight I spy a car I had my eye on a few weeks back, now returned. She is a late 80's Civic—*hi miles, but runs great.* The price has even dropped to $600. Not the car I imagine covering the entire distance up the Alaska Highway, though something in her headlights suggests she would die trying.

I turn to see my archenemy smirking at me. Not coincidentally smirking and looking at me at the same time, but smirking *right* at me. He has caught me eyeing this piece of shit car and agrees with me. *Yes,* he says, *you and that car are a perfect match, completely deserving of each other.* I swear he knows that the available balance on my credit card could only get me the car, cheap insurance and perhaps three tanks of gas. *After that?* his smirk asks. Then he goes back to his book.

As the bus groans through the stop, I change the order of my plan. I will pop my archenemy in the nose first. Everything will just have to fall into place afterwards. I will walk up and smack him in his smarmy face.

No, I cannot and I know it. I think the act would be basic assault and battery, which a rudimentary knowledge of cop shows tells me is illegal. Word would cross the street and my boss and coworkers would watch me closely. No one wants a loose cannon behind a three-hundred-pound Sharp AR C250A copier. No more would I be able to get cocoa and danishes from the Java

House. I would be banned from the bus, forcing me to walk the three miles to work. The latter two might even cause me to lose some of my extra thirty pounds. Or I would be forced to go buy that car, and go broke or wherever else it wanted to take me. My world would be forever changed.

I reach up and pull the cord for the next stop. We are no more than three blocks from my $600 Civic. Perhaps some browsing and a walk in the light drizzle will cool me off. Another bus will be by in a half-hour. I can catch it or maybe have dinner in an unfamiliar restaurant nearby. I saw a small bookstore a few blocks back. Maybe they sell atlases.

I rise into the aisle and let the bus's slowing carry me forward. My hands sing in my jacket pockets. My hands—the one I would use to punch my archenemy, the one I will write with when I start again, the two I would use to grip the Civic's steering wheel—they positively hum.

My archenemy senses me coming and looks up. His eyes betray the smallest amount of concern. He knows this is not my stop. He knows something is happening. He knows who I am.

FOOL'S GOLD

We first met D.B. Cooper in October, our third month down south. We fell for him immediately. He was sly, friendly and laughed easier than one would expect from a federal fugitive. We realized early on he was not *the* D.B. Cooper, and later learned he wasn't even *a* D.B. Cooper, but rather a native local who between delusions collected a paycheck from the nearby mill under the name Samuel Stirratt.

"Let me know if he's bothering you," the bartender said to me in a hush when D.B. sidled up close to Laura. I waved him off with a nod of thanks. We moved to this land of Bigfoot and volcanoes with high hopes. Mr. Cooper was the first true ray to shine since our arrival.

"So that was you?" Laura said. She followed with an elaborate hand gesture meant to symbolize his skyjacking adventure. He recognized it.

"My little escapade." He grinned and threw back his Lucky Lager with an aloof flair. "The follies of our youth."

"You've changed your look," I said. "No more sunglasses and short hair?"

He pulled a wrinkled hand through graying hair hanging a little too close to the collar. "Gotta keep up with the times. Can't just stick with what worked in the glory days."

Laura leaned back and took him in. He was about the right age, but his unkempt hair and weathered hickory shirt and jeans didn't suggest a man with a plan. Laura smiled like she hadn't in months and put the lightest of hands on his thin shoulder.

"So you got away with it."

He shrugged innocently, but added an ulterior grin.

"Gettin' away with it once ain't the trick, sweetie. It's gettin' away with it every day after that."

He settled in and gave us the lowdown on his scheme. True, he admitted, he grew up in this area and most knew him by another name, but then what better cover? He'd spent his childhood exploring the very woods he touched down in that rainy night in 1971. He knew the trails, the creeks and their runs, and how the authorities would go about looking for him. He may as well have parachuted into his own bed, he said, in which he was tucked safely by the time the helicopters, dogs and spotlights came calling.

"He's full of shit, y'know," the bartender said when D.B. excused himself to the restroom. Laura just said, "We're fine, thanks."

Growing up in Seattle, just three hours north of that bar, I had been required by a high school state history class to do a report on a local historical figure. While others chose Doc Maynard, the Denny family or Jack Sikma, I opted for our barmate that night. That report was fifteen years gone but I remembered enough to notice his inaccuracies. Our friend claimed he stored his stolen million in various places in the surrounding woods, though the actual amount was $200,000. He talked of watching the stars roll by during his fall, but the real drop occurred on a rainy November night. Finally he called himself D.B. The ticket had been purchased under the name Dan Cooper, later misquoted and immortalized by a law officer. I considered impressing Laura with how much of that report I retained, but knew she wasn't interested. Over our seasons together we'd met plenty of people who brimmed with bullshit. Given the choice between them and someone devoid of bullshit, we knew to choose the former. They were probably lying, but at least they had something interesting to say.

D.B. appeared surprised at our still being there when he returned from the bathroom. He smiled widely.

"I've been doing all the talking," he said. "Where are you kids from?"

Laura and I looked at each other—for years we took

pride in our inability to answer that question.

"I guess we're from here now," I said. "In July we moved into a house just north of the river. Off Jefferson Road past the Cayhill farm. It belongs to my uncle, Jim Stepley."

D.B. nodded. "I know the place. Before that?"

"We moved down from Alaska."

He stretched his scratchy jaw into an admiring nod. "Looking for gold?"

"Sort of," I said. "We worked the summers up there, shaking the gold out of cruise ships and tour buses."

D.B. grinned. "Smart. The only reliable treasure—gullible people. But I've heard winters up there are tough."

Laura ordered another round. "We usually went somewhere else for the winter."

"Mostly tourist traps," I added. "Ski towns, the coast, wherever struck us in the fall."

D.B. gave a gentleman's thanks when Laura paid for his fresh Lucky. "Very interesting. But what are you doing in Battle Ground?"

"Laura got a job as an assistant director of a studio down in Portland," I said, knowing Laura disliked talking about her new job. She liked it less each time someone asked. "She paints."

"An artist?" He eyed her in a way that, were he twenty years younger, would've caused me honest concern.

"I haven't done anything in a long time," she said. "Six months, maybe a year."

"Still," he said. "I'd love to see your work sometime."

Like a schoolgirl, she couldn't even make eye contact.

"Sure. That would be nice."

He showed no interest in my occupation. Having mailed out three resumes that morning, I felt thankful.

"Battle Ground is a bit of a drive from Portland, though," he said.

"Paul's uncle offered us the place up here for cheap," Laura told him. "And we wanted to bring our little girl up in a small town."

I pulled the picture from my wallet before D.B. could even express his joy at our procreating.

"Baby Tallulah," I said. "She's with a sitter. This is our first real night out since we moved here."

"Tallulah." He held the photo up in the bar's dying light and then handed it back. "Simply beautiful."

"We didn't want to raise her in the city," Laura said. "Places on the edge tend to produce something a little different."

I nodded towards our barmate. "Case in point."

Cooper couldn't deny it.

"Yeah, Battle Ground's a great little town. But still, she's changing."

He glanced around the bar, suddenly lost for words. Flashy microbrews were on tap, relegating his bottles of Lucky Lager to a small fridge below the bar. Like us, Cooper had passed by the shiny SUVs lining the parking lot. He either didn't feel or ignored the condescendingly-healthy looks that came our way each time he lit up a cigarette, in this bar he'd been drinking in for thirty years.

"I just don't know if a guy could get away with a good skyjacking around this new crowd," he said, smiling sidelong at us. "You kids, though, you're alright."

Laura took my hand and squeezed hard enough to pop my knuckles.

A little after nine-thirty Laura shifted back against me in her familiar way to say she was ready to go. As we rose, Mr. Cooper's arthritic knees stopped him just short of a full curtsey.

"Kids, it has been wonderful."

"Likewise, D.B." I shook his hand. Laura offered up her cheek and Mr. Cooper delivered a peck soft as a first snow.

After a few steps, Laura turned back.

"One thing—that money they found a few years back..."

He shrugged like a kid with his hand in the cookie jar.

"Planted, I confess. My own doing."

Laura smiled. "To remind them you were out there?"

D.B. shook his head. "To remind myself to keep running." He raised his beer. "My regards to Tallulah."

Our back porch afforded only a view of a small stream feeding into the Lewis River beyond the trees, and we needed to trudge a few hundred feet through the overgrown brush for a view of Mount Hood and St. Helens on the days they were out. On nights when the rains let up, Laura liked to take her wine out on the porch and talk about the things she missed most.

She began small at first. Meals available only at certain restaurants, the loose and chiming fun of dancing a summer night away to a bar band made up of acquaintances, or a smile which can only be given by an odd friend with too few teeth on a cold winter day. I would nod in agreement at each one and fill in small details she had forgotten. Early on I said things like, "But we're here now and we're going to do fine," and other disingenuous crap until I sounded like a bad motivational speaker pushing a series of inspirational videos on late night TV. She would shrug off my concerns and call her musings therapeutic, so I backed off. I often hauled Tallulah out, knowing somehow she needed to hear this, though she simply giggled and smiled occasionally. The parallels of our involvement were not lost on Laura.

Slowly her reflections became more general. One November night she missed the seasons the most. Not the traditional four, but the two that mattered most to those who worked them—summer and winter, high-season and off-season. I asked what she missed about them and she said everything. She missed the opening up in the spring—pulling plywood off storefront windows, studying cruise ship schedules, old friends returning for one more go around, invariably someone's last. She missed the end of the season, watching a place wind down like a giant jet engine, the exchanging of upcoming plans and contact information with friends and promises to remain in touch. She missed that sweet spot in the heart of a summer, a two-month hurricane's eye when you were settled into your apartment and your work. All was good and six weeks remained before you had to start thinking about packing your belongings into your truck and finding somewhere else to go and something else to do for the next six months.

"The seasons here simply move on without us," she said. "They don't force us anywhere. Maybe it's just this mild climate. The winters aren't too cold, the summers aren't too hot. There's no reason to go."

"Did we ever need a reason in eight years?" I said, risking my position of indifferent observer. She also realized the danger of both of us starting down that path. She took my hand and offered me her wine in a way that said I could finish the glass and down the whole bottle and she'd love me all the more.

"I don't know if I want anything back." She looked down to where a light rain shaded the far off hills. "I just *miss* every once in a while. Is there anything wrong with that?"

"Nothing," I said.

I took a sip and handed her wine back. Tallulah was

asleep but I moved her closer to watch the rain run off the overhang onto the deck. Her eyes stayed closed but I still wanted her to smell and hear these things. I had an odd hunch they were important.

I never pretended to understand Laura's art. She began drawing and painting years before we met and would doubtlessly continue doing so whether or not my untrained eye was present with simplistic verdicts such as "I like it" or "Not my favorite." I didn't know if she really understood her work either, how she took the world into her eyes, broke it down and then reassembled it onto paper or canvas. She'd always disliked talking about her art. Discussions usually devolved into pseudo-intellectuals trying to label her or others asking why she couldn't just paint something how it really looked. Once, on a long-gone mountain evening after too much beer, I attempted eloquence and told her how her paintings put solid lines into the world where nature would if it didn't have to deal with the little details that screw everything up. She simply said "Thank you," and kissed me for the rest of the night. Figuring I could never top that evening, I stopped trying.

Over our years together Laura's paintings served many purposes, from birthday gifts for friends to rent payments for a landlord who loved her work. Slowly she began to get in local galleries, supplementing our income and elevating herself from seasonal nomad to struggling artist. Other people's words, of course. Laura saw herself only as a girl drawing the world the way she wished it looked.

She hadn't painted much since moving to Battle Ground. This despite having her first real studio, a modified den facing our overgrown backyard. Before she had created wherever space allowed—in the living room or kitchen, or out on a patio when living somewhere the weather permitted it. She cited time issues—primarily her new job and Tallulah—but I knew the pressure of a designated creative space intimidated her. If one happened to assemble a car in their garage, it was a pleasant surprise. Build a factory and people expected Corvettes and Cadillacs. Her new job couldn't be overlooked, though.

"Grading other people's creativity saps my own," she often said when opening her evening wine. She would pour a glass and poke her head into the studio. Sooner than later she headed out onto the deck to tell Tallulah and the trees about the things she missed most.

In hopes of inspiring her, I uncrated and hung a few pieces from her last project—a series of mountain paintings inspired, as near as she could tell, by a winter in southwest Colorado. They were mountains of the like I had never seen before, and bore almost no resemblance to their supposed muse of the jagged San Juans. These mountains consisted of so much more than rocks and dirt, and no roads or trails traversed them. With Laura's lines I saw no way of ever getting into them. If I could, though, I knew I would walk in to those mountains and never leave.

We were fearless once, Laura and I. We weren't out there BASE jumping or skydiving, but not much scared us. We didn't worry about not having insurance or not knowing where we would be living or working in six months. We didn't worry about not having a house or a retirement plan when our college newsletters told us about fellow alumnus getting a big promotion or becoming senior manager of this or that. The world didn't frighten us. We stood alone in that stupid and beautiful bravery of discovering someone else, perhaps longer than we had right. Still, if two people have never felt at some time that they had one up on everyone and everything else, I would be wary to say they were ever truly in love.

I met Laura eight summers ago in Juneau. I tended bar at the Red Dog Saloon and she pushed Rie Muñoz paintings at a gallery on Franklin Street. We were freshly liberated from higher learning and had both come north with the simple notion of seeing a little country. She showed me her paintings and we hiked the local trails until two in the morning and fell into a fragile love unique to summer in the higher latitudes. Some friends headed off to wholesome and productive destinations at summer's end—jobs, internships or further schooling. But others spoke of wintering in sunny places and ski towns with names exotic as mixed drinks when compared to the light beers of the more traditional winter plans. We bit and headed to Key West on the advice of a friend we'd known for two months. We soon found ourselves happily locked in a cycle with the seasons, working as bartenders, tour guides, cooks, deckhands or whatever came up. We kept the tourist towns of Alaska as a summer constant, relying on the guaranteed work and good money to stock up for whatever winter plans we dreamed up. We were happy, paying our own way and figured no one had a right to complain. With her family in Bellingham and mine in Seattle, we simply passed through the Puget Sound during the fall and spring to deposit various knickknacks in parents' garages and allow family to check our vital statistics and make thinly veiled pleas for us to come to our senses. *It'd be so nice to see you kids more than once every six months. Your brother says they're hiring at Microsoft...*

Each spring and fall we welcomed old friends like familiar perennials. We communicated in the off-seasons through postcards at first and later e-mail, crossing paths for six months here and there. In the last few years several found permanent homes and seemed legitimately happy. We simply kept moving, figuring we would get some sign when the time came to stop.

The first sign came as frequent morning sickness in July of the previous summer. The final irrefutable proof arrived shiny and crying at 4:32 am on a March day in Anchorage. Needless to say, many things changed. When Laura was pregnant we spoke of continuing our movement, and simply forcing the forthcoming baby to keep up. Perhaps wandering would be ingrained in her genetics, since near as we could tell she was conceived in a sleeping bag in the back of our Four Runner while driving the Alcan north that June. But when she arrived, fresh from arguably her biggest move, her small pink and shaking form demanded some sort of stability. Our families agreed.

"A steady home is what a child needs," they took turns saying. "Not to be packed in a suitcase every six months and hauled a thousand miles."

The logistics of our kinetic life, they insisted, would endanger Tallulah's well-being. She might be accidentally boxed up and left all winter in a storage shed, or simply lost in the shuffle like the small electronic PDA my father gave me for Christmas two years ago, about which I never heard the end. Then there was the issue of money. And hospital bills. And a real home. And college. And braces, though presently she possessed only three teeth, all of them in my opinion straight. Despite our nomadic tendencies, we dutifully deposited each season's take every six months in a savings account at a Wells Fargo branch a few blocks from my parents' home in Ballard. Just as we learned growing up—work hard and put money in the bank. But we soon found there were 401K's, IRA's, CD's and a host of other acronymic options we were fools for not exploring. Our antiquated notion of simply making and saving money was only one step better than burying it in coffee cans in the backyard.

Two months after Tallulah's birth, we caved. We called the gallery owners in Seattle who the summer before had great success with Laura's prints. At the time they mentioned opening a Portland gallery with an emphasis on Northwest artists, and they would be looking for an assistant director. It offered everything we'd been told we lacked—retirement, health benefits and so on—all a convenient yet safe distance from family. When my uncle offered his rental home in nearby Battle Ground, we agreed the cosmos were aligning to seal the deal. Portland struck us as an honest and real city, a hard-working blue-collar stepbrother to Seattle's Starbucks-swilling techno-yuppies. And we wouldn't be living in Portland proper, but rather *Battle Ground*, Washington. The name alone gave us hope and spawned visions of fields still smoldering with the genuine carnage of an epic confrontation.

Despite the promising moniker, last July our U-Haul rolled into an assemblage of strip malls and housing developments dropped like a soup stain onto the quaint downtown and surrounding farmland. Completely recovered from whatever skirmish the name derived from, Battle Ground now peacefully housed displaced urbanites with big off-road rigs they washed at the first signs of dirt. They commuted to nearby white-collar jobs and spent the weekends working in their yards and chairing neighborhood groups hoping to bring to Battle Ground the sterilized outdoors of an L.L. Bean ad.

My uncle's house rested mercifully on the town's northern outskirts, convenient to the Safeway but safely on the rural fringe. Laura started work and I stayed at home with Tallulah, taking part-time bartending jobs at nearby places on the weekends. In an attempt to satisfy my parents, I searched for work to make use of my journalism degree. With ten years and countless blue-collar jobs between myself and my education, I was faced with a task not unlike trying to sell a beaten used car I had previously planned on simply driving until it died. I eventually took a position copyediting three afternoons a week at a local newspaper. The publication was a safe and friendly local affair, where a spelling bee or large brush fire earned front page above the fold. The reporters were dutiful if not idealistic, with

71

heroes leaning closer to Dave Barry and Erma Bombeck than Hunter S. Thompson or Edward R. Murrow. To their credit, their grammar was exceptional.

So we settled in and did things a Northwest mom and dad and baby do. We spent rainy afternoons up at the zoo, and explored the science exhibits at OMSI that would be old-hat when Tallulah was old enough to understand them. We took her to the coast to sit on wet logs on a rocky beach and pointed out the bigger waves and what I hoped were whales. We bought a sturdy baby backpack at GI Joe's and strapped her on and hiked around the Gorge and through the Ape Caves in the shadow of Mount St. Helens. We took trips to Seattle and let our parents take turns ogling Tallulah and smiling proudly when we left early Sunday afternoon due to work looming on Monday morning. We did what we hoped was best.

One uncommonly warm February evening Laura arrived home from the store with two sacks of groceries and D.B. Cooper.

"Look who I bumped into at Safeway." She led him into the kitchen. We'd returned to the bar several times since October and observed Mr. Cooper in various stages of inebriation. One evening found him so far along he more or less recreated our first encounter. It had been a pleasant one, so we let the night run its course. I never imagined him existing outside that bar, and now he stood in my kitchen putting my Grape Nuts away. It was odd, a little scary and wonderful.

"Please join us for dinner," Laura said. "It won't take long."

"Oh, I don't want to impose," D.B. said. "I just wanted to say hello."

"We insist," I said.

He scratched his head, considering whatever business he had planned. When he removed his hand, his unwashed hair stood of its own accord.

"Okay, but only if Tallulah says it's okay."

I introduced him to our daughter and the two studied each other in equal volleys of amazement. Eventually she entrusted him with the noise that we assumed to be her first word, either "dog" or "bog." We gathered around plates of Laura's enchiladas, our guest eyeing his glass of wine as if it held some trendy concoction he felt wary of lending his full trust. I found him a Lucky Lager in the garage and D.B. started telling us the history of our house. He spoke of its days as home to a prolific still and Battle Ground's finest homemade hooch. Then of the time in the sixties when a rural doctor set up a makeshift hospital here at his home while waiting for the local clinic to be built. D.B. himself had an ingrown toenail removed in the very room we were eating in, close to where the sour cream sat.

"Wow," Laura said. "Paul's uncle didn't tell us anything about all that stuff."

I agreed. My uncle did, however, tell us enough that we both knew Mr. Cooper was lying to beat the band. Nonetheless, the structure's true history—built in 1968, home to my uncle until 1992 and rented sporadically since—paled in comparison, so we let the skyjacker carry on. It was much finer entertainment than the syndicated reruns of *Everybody Loves Raymond* that usually prattled on during dinner.

After dinner D.B. was so full he had only energy enough to lie about the history of one more room, the den *nee* studio. It was once a brothel of sorts, but he didn't go into great detail as Tallulah watched him closely from Laura's cocked hip.

"Wow." He stepped up to look deep into Laura's mountain paintings. "I've never seen anything like these before."

"Thank you." Unlike too many fragile artists, she could take a true compliment.

"Where is that?"

"Nowhere, really," she said. "I painted them when we lived in Colorado for a winter."

"I've been there." D.B. studied the paintings. "My cousin moved down to Montrose and I drove with him in an old Buick."

"Actually, you're right." I shared a look of surprise with Laura. "We were up the road a bit, toward Telluride."

D.B. laughed and snapped his fingers so delightfully loud I expected a wrinkled digit to drop on the floor. "I knew it. Yeah, I made that trip almost twenty-five years ago. Took us almost a week. That piece of crap Buick musta broke down ten times. Yeah..."

He trailed off in a way that made me wish I'd been riding along in the Buick. We let him enjoy his silent recollection until he jolted from it with a start.

"That's my favorite." The painting he pointed to showed mountains running with mineral veins far too bright and shiny to blame on nature. Their artificial beauty made my teeth ache.

"It's called 'Fool's Gold,'" Laura said.

The name made him smile more. "Yeah?"

Laura shifted Tallulah to her other hip and stepped up between D.B. and the painting.

"I always saw Telluride as this beautiful little town being worn like bad trendy clothes by all the rich people who vacationed there. Like those hats…"

"California cowboy hats," I said, recalling her favorite self-coined expression.

"Yes." She turned to Mr. Cooper. "You know those cowboy hats with the bands covered in bad Southwestern patterns drawn by white artists down in Taos and made of fabric all starchy and firm enough to cut bread? No dirt on them whatsoever? You know the ones I mean?"

D.B. obviously didn't but enjoyed her tirade. He nodded vigorously.

"Well, that's how the town hit me," she said. "It's authentic and real and rich in a *true* way, like an old honest cowboy hat. But those people drag into town and bastardize it like those fancy hats. They fly in on private jets dripping with money and jewels and billboard smiles and snotty kids in Abercrombie and Fitch clothes who just scowl at everything. They can't see how poor they really are, even with the damn mountains screaming it down at them."

Laura stopped for a breath. D.B. just leaned back and crossed his arms. I joined him. I hadn't seen this girl in a while and missed her greatly.

"I knew there was a reason I liked this one," D.B. said.

Laura handed me Tallulah. I feared she might start apologizing for her diatribe, but instead pulled the painting down from the wall and held it out to our fugitive houseguest.

"Take it."

He instinctively unfolded his arms, but didn't take the painting.

"I couldn't." ·

"I insist." Laura forced the canvas toward him until he wrapped his weathered hands around the edges like glass. "No one else gets it but you."

"I get it," I said, though I knew not like D.B.

"You have to," she said. "You're married to me. And maybe with it gone I'll be inspired to do something to replace it. Take it and enjoy it."

Mr. Cooper stared hard down at the painting. "I can't let you do that, honey."

"You can't stop me, either."

"You better take it," I said. "Angry artists are no fun."

He finally bowed his head, as if doffing a cap he didn't wear. I retrieved a plastic garbage bag and pried the painting from D.B.'s hands to prep it for traveling. One didn't sell art in the Northwest and not learn to keep it dry. D.B. watched with the nervous eyes of a new parent. When I returned his painting, his eyes lit up and he snapped his fingers again in his bone-cracking style.

"We'll make it an honest deal," he said. "Got a pen and paper?"

Laura pulled both from the hall desk. Mr. Cooper sat at the dinner table and scribbled for a few dramatic minutes. His only breaks came as a couple chuckles and the occasional million-mile gaze into his own memory. He finally stood and folded the paper into itself several times. The end product bordered on origami.

"Here you go." He handed the paper to Laura. "Keep it somewhere safe."

Laura examined the cluster of paper.

"It's a map," he said.

"To what?" I said.

He only grinned and retook his painting with a new sureness.

"Oh, you know. I trust you'll know when to use it."

Laura clutched the map close to her breast.

"Just in case," she said.

D.B. Cooper nodded. "Just in case." He held up the painting. "Thank you, kids, for the whole evening."

With that, he ducked out into a night rain shower and rattled off in his truck. Laura refused to let me see the folded paper until I promised not to open it. Later that night she placed the paper on a shelf in her studio and even painted a little over the next couple of nights. Though we never talked about that map, we both knew we had no business touching it.

In March, Tallulah's first birthday came as solid rain and wind, and found Laura and her wine on the back porch with the birthday girl. That night the thing Laura missed most was the parrot at the Crabwalk Café who didn't bite.

We wintered in the islands three years ago, living a block from the water in a little apartment we rented at admittedly high gringo rates. Like everyone fresh to the islands we made plans to never leave, forgot them, and spent our time off getting sunburned and drinking Medalla beer. The Crabwalk Café was a little open-air affair down on the waterfront. The café offered pressed Cuban sandwiches, the island's only Italian sodas, and two white parrots perched permanently near the front gate. A sign hung beneath them. ONE OF US BITES—TRY US AND FIND OUT WHICH ONE. Laura leaned down to explain all this to Tallulah.

"You would stick you finger out, Lula, and *snap.*" Laura took one of Tallulah's tiny hands between her fingers. "That other little crapper would snap it every time."

Tallulah, groggy from her rich chocolate cake and unfamiliar with the vice-like grip of a parrot, simply giggled.

"Why don't you miss him, too?" I said.

Laura eyed me warily. "Because it took all winter for your fingernail to grow back."

Tonight I had my own wine and drank liberally.

"Okay, but would you appreciate the one who didn't bite if the biter wasn't there?"

Her glass was empty and she took mine, eyeing me like a questionable ally, or just a guy who couldn't hold his liquor.

"You still don't know the rules of my game, do you?"

I could only say no. She set her wine glass down between us and watched the grays, blacks and greens of the evening sky duel in the distance.

"Fine," she said. "I miss it all."

"Me, too."

I took her hand and held it until both my girls fell asleep to the sound of the rain.

April came in with more sun and warmth than it had right, and daylight savings time sent sunset later into the night, after Tallulah's bedtime. On those radiant orange nights Laura missed all our friends the most. I was done fighting. Truth be told, I now looked forward to these nights as I imagined families gathered around the radio in the days before television.

She would put one of her old mixed tapes on the little portable player, fat with John Hiatt and Townes Van Zandt and honest stuff like that, and rattle off names. Jim down on the docks, the Timms brothers from the train, Erin at the dive shop, Tony the lounge-singing cook, Albie the helicopter pilot who wrote poetry on the glaciers between flights, and Crazy Stan—never clinically diagnosed but obvious even to laymen. She allowed a pause between each name to properly draw up memories and for us to laugh or sigh or shake our heads. Sometimes we talked about them individually, but mostly I just waited in anticipation for the next name. Though we never verbalized it, in each pause and chuckle we wondered where these people were now and why none settled here in the middle. None of them possessed or wanted the strength to hold on to the world's big merry-go-round, and the societal centrifuge had flung them safely off to the fringe. It worried me that, between the three of us, Laura, Tallulah and I might have that strength.

Legally speaking, we were not friendless in Battle Ground. There were people who recognized us at Fred Meyer and waved at red lights and told us we looked well. Early on they came from Laura's work, though the other gallery employees dwelled primarily among the expensive overgrown greenery of Lake Oswego and the West Hills. They preferred downtown restaurants with twenty-dollar appetizers, waiting lists and Cary Grant-esque waiters who enjoyed serving us far too much to be trusted. When conversation strayed from work, it did so like a truck tire from a worn groove in heavy snow—most often things simply felt sloppy, but complete disaster was never far away.

My work provided even fewer prospects. My only real interaction came from a twenty-something intern who listened only to Phish and Mingus and saw me as the lone person at the paper who might supply him some narcotics. We shared what became an incredibly awkward lunch at McMenamins. Upon realizing my drug supply offered only PediaCare, Gold Bond Baby Powder and some leftover 222's for Laura's occasional migraine, he immediately stopped orbiting my cubicle.

The bulk of the people we now saw were young couples with which we shared only the commonality of procreation. Many acquaintances stemmed from PlayPark, an over-engineered monstrosity of good intentions sprouting out of the greenbelt near town. It bore tunnels and bridges and other designs meant to challenge developing minds, and paths designed to help them navigate the hurdles life would throw at them soon enough. It proudly held the logos of the software firms who funded the park with the apparent goal of engineering adolescent development down to a three-month course. The border offered a viewing area from which parents could dote. Each time we went we inevitably met someone who knew the couple we met the week before, who lived down the street from the couple the week before that. We would then be invited to another barbeque or birthday party on the premise that it was the polite thing to do, as all the people we hardly knew would be there. We were wary to talk too much at these functions. Deep down we both feared we might be joining this same crowd for T-ball, soccer practice and school plays for decades to come. We would need to pace ourselves.

I began a lazy boycott of PlayPark, but Laura continued dutifully. Tallulah was taking more steps every day and babbled with great assuredness. Laura didn't want her falling even a week behind developmentally. The swarm of new mothers swept her into their oddly competitive maternities, curious for small details about everyone, Laura included. Was she breastfeeding? What made us choose Tallulah as a name, and was she coming along on schedule? Did I make good money at the paper? If not, one of their husbands might be able to get me on at Hewlett Packard or something of the like. She began attending PlayPark solely out of fear for the backbiting frenzy she saw bestowed on whichever mother didn't show up on any given day. *I mean, I like her and all, but I think her little girl is just a little out of control, have you noticed? She needs to get on Atkins—it's been a year since the baby and she hasn't taken off the weight. Don't think her husband hasn't noticed…*

"They're like a sewing circle," Laura would say. "Except not a damn one of them can even sew."

Gender programming left me to befriend the husbands, who all proved as reliable and boring as a short stack of pancakes. Most were in their late twenties or early thirties and accepted marriage and fatherhood with the same helplessness they used for the few pounds creeping on each year. They laughed easily but defensively, and took comfort in the restraints of family life. They wore nothing but casual slacks and golf shirts bearing their company logos, even in the evening and on the weekends. They subscribed to *Golf Digest* and *Robb Report* and actually looked forward to reading the articles. They did all this and more of their own accord. I realized I must watch myself carefully around these men.

So these were our new friends, and our old ones were relegated to those evening talks and the occasionally overnight stop in Portland on their way to somewhere else. It hardly seemed fair to anyone involved. We could share so much information with some people—who had an episiotomy, how much people paid for their homes, whose spouses drank to excess, and so on—and not know a damn thing about them. At the same time we could be completely ignorant of an old friend's last name, hometown or other vital statistics, but still felt we knew them deeply, and that we ourselves were known.

We arrived at the bar that night just in time to see them taking D.B. Cooper away. In the end it wouldn't be federal offenses bringing him down, but just a good old-fashioned drunk and disorderly.

"I wasn't doing anything wrong," he demanded.

A severely stylish lady in short pants and an expensive blouse near the door struck a pose begging to differ. Her partner, a square-jawed pile of muscle packed into a pressed khaki shirt, stood nearby with his big forearms crossed. He looked as stern as one could with so much hair gel. A young state trooper sauntered over to get her side of the story. It came in sighs, eye rolls and hair flips. The trooper's partner stood with D.B. near the back of the cruiser, the lights popping but mercifully silent. That trooper looked far less interested in our fugitive's story, and fitted him with a set of handcuffs.

All this was far more interesting than anything inside the bar, despite the recent addition of a Golden Tee golf video game and a CD jukebox with modern adult contemporary hits. The patrons flanked the police cruiser like spectators unsure of who exactly was the home team. The owner came out, squinting in the sun, and joined the officer and the J. Crew couple. I eavesdropped and heard phrases like *problem drinker*, *harassment*, and *changing clientele* before I tired of listening. Laura just stared at the officer questioning D.B.

"I was just talking," D.B. said. "Getting to know people.

Ain't that what bars are for?"

"Not in the way you do it, sir. I need your identification. May I see your wallet?"

D.B. huffed. "Not enough room in my wallet with all my money. That and I don't have it on me. I never carry it. Personal reasons. 'Sides, everyone here knows me."

The young officer shifted his weight to his other hip and made his overloaded utility belt creak.

"Well, I live here and I don't know you. This is really just a formality, sir, and you're making it take longer than necessary." The trooper fumbled at his belt, bypassing the mace and flashlight and gun for a pad and pen. "Full legal name and address, please."

D.B. squared his shoulders, but still looked very frail.

"I'm not required to tell you anything."

The trooper sighed. "It'll mean the difference between eating dinner at home or with us tonight."

D.B.'s shoulders dropped. He was about to speak when he noticed Laura. He didn't want to say anything and we didn't want to hear anything. In his faded grey eyes I saw where we all wanted him to be—thirty years younger, tumbling down, down, down through a stinging November rain, unsure of where he would land but knowing wherever he came down, he would find his way home and they would never ever catch him.

"Full name and address, sir?"

D.B. Cooper dropped his eyes to the dirt. They landed with no parachute.

"Stirratt. Samuel Stirratt. 1532 Edmonds Road. Battle Ground, Washington."

The young officer took down the information and opened the cruiser's back door. The skyjacker got inside and stared straight forward.

"I'm not thirsty anymore." Laura turned and walked away. Our car actually sat parked on the opposite side of the lot, but I knew she wasn't walking towards anything. I knew I should take all this in for a moment, as this might be the last time I saw a lot of these things. Instead I turned and followed my wife.

I think Laura cried a little on the way home, but I didn't look too close. She stared out her side window at blurred trees, mailboxes and the always-coming rain. Some tears beg to be noticed, and then there is crying people don't want anyone else to see. God help those who can't tell the difference. I tread around Laura's like dynamite caps.

Laura was out of the Four Runner before I killed the engine, making a beeline inside and leaving the front door open behind her. By the time I entered, Laura was out the back door with Tallulah in one arm and a half-full bottle of local wine, recorked from three nights earlier. The babysitter, a corn-fed teenage girl from a farm down the road, looked to me wide-eyed.

"I wasn't doing anything," she pleaded but still sounded guilty. I had simply assumed she regularly pilfered our beer and snuck in a boyfriend on our nights out. Growing up in Battle Ground she had earned those things in addition to the $30 we paid her. I assured her all was well and made up a lie about Laura simply being upset because some movie she wanted to see was sold out. I paid her a full night's wages and she made a hushed call from our hall phone. An oversized pickup soon rumbled up and whisked her away, though probably not too far.

I took a lone plastic cup out onto the deck for myself, knowing Laura's anger drank straight from the bottle. Laura hadn't yet uncorked the bottle, but rather rocked Tallulah in her arms and sang our little girl a song about Christmas in prison. I opened the bottle and filled my cup. The wine was flat, ice cold and delicious.

Laura finished her song and Tallulah opened her eyes. Raindrops hit our overhang with a sound that always made her smile. Laura set Tallulah down on her feet, and she started a Frankenstein-like walk across the deck. When her toes hit the open wet planks, she looked back at us and grinned.

"She likes the rain," I said, knowing damn well Laura knew it already.

Laura nodded and looked skyward. "That and the way the wind howls through this shoddy roof job of your uncle's."

It was true. The winter east winds from the Gorge made me think the whole roof would lift right off, but it put our little girl out every night.

After a minute, Tallulah yawned and strode back to Laura. I made her a bed of blankets next to our chairs and we sat and talked about the noises we missed the most. I talked about the metal roar of the Ballard Locks and how Johnny Cash songs forever reminded me of the afternoons my dad and his union friends needed the back porch for unwinding. Laura talked about the furnace in her parents' home that started like a diesel engine each night, or how a good Alaskan morning drizzle on her day off gave her permission to stay in bed all day. Tallulah shifted several times and giggled—mostly up at the rain, but I hoped a little at her folks.

"Do you think she'll remember all this?" Laura said. "The rain? The roof? All this stuff that makes her feel safe?"

I had found the bottom of my third cup of wine and knew it would've been wise to retire, maybe kiss each of my girls on the forehead and head inside to bed. But I felt pretty gone on the wine and a respite from the evening showers was just settling over us. I may not have been the best father, but I knew not to pass up a break in the rain when you're feeling high.

"I don't know, baby," I said. "I hope she feels safe. But I don't know if she is, really. I think there are things we don't see that are after her. And the things we're trying to protect her from will get her whether we want them to or not."

Laura leaned across and tipped my plastic cup so she could see all the way down to the bottom. She stood and crossed her arms.

"So what do you propose we do?"

I took my own look down into my empty cup.

"I guess I should suggest we call it a night, hit the sack and get up to do the best we can tomorrow," I said. "But I really think we should grab that little girl and anything we think is important and run. It's just coming up on May and the season's starting up north. If we go now and stay smart, they'll never catch us."

She smiled like gold, touched my shoulder and disappeared inside. I rubbed Tallulah's sleeping leg with my foot and woke her up. It was no longer raining but she still grinned and grinned. She didn't look completely safe, but she sure didn't look worried.

I looked up to see Laura standing over us. She held D.B. Cooper's map in her hand. The paper was open and she smiled wide as a summer moon.

"Okay," she said. "Let's go."

WINDFALL

I came to know them all through donuts. Good donuts, arguably Juneau's best, prepared and served exclusively at the Drift-In Store near the airport where I clerked. I played no role in the baking nor harbored any secret recipes, but merely guided the tongs to the pastries as directed by customers. We sold other things—snack chips, prepackaged sandwiches and large fountain drinks—and even rented videos, but the donuts' following rivaled that of an underground rock band.

The Hove brothers ate only traditional jelly-filled and claimed to be part native, though the percentage varied from ¼ to 1/16 dependent on the company. They fancied themselves urban thugs and hoped a hint of ethnicity would strengthen their credentials. In my short retail encounters with them, buying accompanying cartons of whole milk and grabbing fistfuls of napkins for inevitable jelly spills, they revealed themselves as simply dumb white bullies. If Wal-Mart sold street toughs, Sam and Scotty Hove would run $9.99 each or $17.99 for the pair.

Wyatt and Melinda took their pastries later in the day when the prices halved, their choices made by what the morning crowd passed over. Wyatt tended bar and rose late. Melinda simply enjoyed sleeping in. The bell above the door rang truer when she entered, and she attacked whatever leftover donut she bought like she'd spent the morning dreaming of it, eating her sweets without girlish caveats—*I really shouldn't, but...* The resultant extra few pounds filled just the right pockets of her Carhartt pants and rounded out her warm face like a good steak. She wasn't beautiful, but that made her attainable, which in turn did make her beautiful. I'd only been off parole for a year, but they hadn't yet written the law I wouldn't consider breaking for her.

Wyatt hailed from money in Vermont, another rich kid on a self-imposed exile from privilege. He arrived in May looking fashionably haggard, and the drinks he served at Hoochies came with cultured smugness. Melinda came to Juneau from Colorado about the same time and the two soon hooked up for the summer, spending nights smoking in Wyatt's apartment near mine in one of the valley's rundown complexes. She had her pilot's license and hopes of flying for the summer, but lacked flight hours and spent the summer loading bags and working the counter for a float plane outfit. She used her extra money to rent a small two-seat Cessna from the local flight school. She threatened once, while choking down an old-fashioned, to take me up there with her.

Now summer was ending. The weather turned a little more each day, the tourist crowds thinned, and seasonal employees were getting laid off. A dusting of snow crested the higher peaks behind downtown on the rare days you could see them. We sold fewer specialty beer six packs and more cases of Budweiser and Coors Light. When people came in for donuts, they got hot chocolate instead of cold milk.

Wyatt and Melinda came to me because I'd been in jail. Real jail, courtesy of the Eastern Oregon Correctional Institution in Pendleton. Most folks in Juneau knew someone who'd served in the town's Lemon Creek Correctional Center, but with alpine scenery in one direction and a Costco visible over the opposite fence, it lacked a certain credibility.

"Maybe we need a gun," Wyatt said as we shared a late breakfast at Donna's Restaurant near the airport. The crowd was thin but still he whispered.

"No, no," Melinda said. "Bad idea."

"That's probably not the best plan," I said. "Besides, I'm the wrong person for that. The government's not big on ex-cons having guns. Check at Fred Meyer, maybe?"

"But I was thinking something with no record, y'know?

Not traceable."

"Guns are serious business." I cut off as our platters arrived. We all feigned a sudden interest in the fall drizzle outside until the waitress left. "I don't know if you want to go down that road."

"I don't want to do anything drastic." Wyatt picked up his fork but didn't eat. "I was just thinking about protection."

"Distance is good protection." Impolite or not, I was hungry and dug into my biscuits and gravy. "The Hoves are just local toughs, probably never been south of Seattle."

Wyatt shook his head and surrendered to his pancakes.

"I can't run. I've made my bed." His B-movie bravado and talk of unregistered guns were a testament to every bad cop show the 1970's produced.

"Or just pay them," I said. "That's what all this is about, right?"

Melinda stopped just short of applause.

"Yes. Listen to him, Wyatt." She grabbed his hand but smiled at me. "He knows about these things."

I steered a chunk of biscuit around my plate with my fork. I had never threatened another man's life or had mine directly threatened. During my short tenure at EOCI I never saw a shiv or lifted weights in the yard, opting instead for TV or books or magazines. I think I heard one man servicing another one night, but I chose to cover my ears with my thin government-issue pillow.

The meek nature of my incarceration matched my crime perfectly. I was the getaway driver in a failed liquor store robbery in Hermiston, a plan hatched over one bottle of off-brand whiskey and carried out with the aid of another. I heard the approaching sirens and performed my assigned duties flawlessly, save for leaving my friend and his empty gun in the store alone and on foot. He rewarded my loyalty by dropping my name in the cruiser's backseat half an hour before his official interrogation began. I received a reduced sentence, bulked up slightly by the car's having been somewhat stolen from his girlfriend for the robbery. My partner and I wound up in Pendleton at the same time though in different cellblocks. We mended fences to a point, but I wasn't expecting any Christmas newsletters or birthday cards.

Of the many who knew me as a convict, only a handful knew this particular truth. Most concluded from my scruffiness and bulk something more violent and criminally respectable. I did little to dispel these assumptions, figuring it my right. If I had to carry an albatross about my neck, I could at least choose the size.

"I told him to call his parents." Melinda removed her hand from his shoulder but left me a trace of the smile. "One Western Union and that would be that."

"Not an option," Wyatt said.

"They bought you that laptop, no questions asked," Melinda said.

"That was if I promised to go to law school this winter."

"You could sell it," I said. "Say it was stolen."

"You wanna buy it?"

I laughed. "I don't know how to work a computer."

"You and this whole damn town." Wyatt pointed his fork at a neighboring hardware. "This place isn't exactly a high tech hotbed. Even if I got cost we'd still be well short."

"Maybe we could borrow the rest," Melinda said.

This sent nervous eyes scattering about the table. After seven months at the Drift-In, I had saved over $900 in a coffee can at the back of my cupboard. I looked forward to opening the second bank account of my life and casually telling my folks I had a little something socked away. If I let Melinda look right at me that coffee can would hang in my eyes.

"I don't know the Hoves real well," I said. "But you might be giving them too much credit." Last March the brothers lowered their beaten Suburban's suspension and installed cruising lights on the undercarriage. A parking lot snow bank soon left them high-centered in a mix of dirty snow and shattered bulbs. Myself and several workers from the neighboring McDonald's finally dislodged them. They tore off and drifted by the next day, humbly quiet and returned to a sensible height. "These aren't the Crips we're talking about."

"The most important thing is a cool head," Melinda said, mopping her plate with toast.

"Oh, now you're all about cool heads." Wyatt laughed sarcastically to the ceiling tiles. "Where was that two days ago?"

I choked back a defense for Melinda. It was not my place, and she was already standing.

"Yeah, let's beat that into the ground. That's productive." She shouldered her bag and tossed a twenty on the table. "I'm off to work. Thanks for meeting with us."

I reflexively grabbed my jacket. I didn't want to be left lunching with a man whose only common ground with me was a fondness for his girlfriend.

"I should go, too, I gotta work at noon." I supplemented her twenty with my pocket's last eight dollars. "Whatever you guys decide, I'll help how I can."

Wyatt nodded without eye contact, but Melinda smiled again. I hoped she knew by *you guys* I meant her, and by *help* I meant I don't know what.

"I knew we could count on you. Some people you can just tell."

Imagine a third grade class reenacting a scene from *Scarface* and you have an idea how all this started. The Hove brothers wanted to play drug dealers, and Melinda and Wyatt wanted to play smugglers. There really wasn't much more to it. Summer's end demanded some kind of entertainment, and a person could only watch so much TV.

Melinda had an acquaintance with some land in Gustavus, a small homesteading community separated from Juneau by fifty miles of mountains and 40-degree waters. Her friend took advantage of his acreage and Gustavus' lack of police to grow whatever struck him. He didn't find much business among his fellow reclusive neighbors—many shared his thinking and horticultural hobbies—and approached Melinda about opportunities in the capital city. Wyatt agreed to do the legwork in town, recognizing a potential pinnacle to his slumming summer and a great tale of romantic rebellion to share with his law school chums.

Wyatt and Melinda heard the Hoves were Juneau's big players as far as distribution—a credit to their ruse—and soon arranged a deal with her Gustavus friend, financed by the Hoves to the tune of several thousand dollars. Melinda took the flight school's Cessna to Gustavus overnight with the intent of filling its empty seat and baggage space with duffels and returning early the next morning, before the flight school personnel arrived for work. She and Wyatt were so attached to the whole arrangement's air of intrigue I didn't have the heart to tell them true smuggling probably required crossing a border or at least a state line. Their plans amounted to little more than taking a Cessna full of weed on a joyride.

On Melinda's return trip, she mistook a Coast Guard helicopter looking for a missing skiff at Barlow Cove as an intercept. She retreated up toward the Herbert Glacier, where her nerves got the best of her and she dropped her cargo out over Windfall Lake north of the Juneau Airport. When she taxied an empty airplane in, Wyatt could only glare from behind the chain link fence.

"Sounds like a natural reaction," I said when they first came to me. "Like what Han Solo did to get himself in trouble with Jabba the Hutt."

The *Star Wars* comparison calmed their Gen-X nerves initially, allowing the two to think themselves a poor man's Han Solo and Princess Leia. I would have preferred the Solo role myself, but with forty extra pounds and shoulders hairier than most, the best I could hope for was a sad and familiar Chewbacca.

Getting the money back from the Gustavus guy was not an option. Melinda's friend was a distrustful recluse who slept with his gun and didn't own a phone. Nothing suggested an abundance of understanding. In his one bright move, Wyatt had given himself a couple days between the transporting and his meeting with the Hoves. This allowed for a complete breakdown, a nervous regrouping, our breakfast, and a trip the next morning to hike the trails around Windfall Lake.

I first heard my new favorite song on the car radio riding out to the trailhead with Melinda and Wyatt. I never learned the song's name, but picked up a few more lines each time I heard it. That day I only remembered the chorus, about letting the wind take your troubles away.

"What's this song?"

Wyatt couldn't have looked more confused when he craned his head back.

"Man, there are more important things at hand here."

He shook his head and silenced the radio. The last two days had made him a moody kind of anxious that I could understand.

Melinda turned the radio back on and placed a calming hand too high up Wyatt's jeans. My song was over.

"It did sound nice," she said, sounding motherly. I felt

childish enough already, in my backseat position straddling the hump of the borrowed Nova's driveshaft. Had Wyatt's erratic driving smacked us into anything too substantial I would break right down the middle of them and out onto the road.

Passing the Auke Bay ferry terminal Melinda asked about me, if I missed my parents down in Pasco and why I'd come north. I answered yes and no to her first question and she laughed. As for the second, it just seemed like something to do.

Even the shaky Wyatt extended an olive branch. "It's a good move. People are cool up here, more understanding of folks in your situation."

Melinda came to both of our rescues.

"Yeah, this is a good place for someone with history."

I fell in love with how her eyes framed those words, because their cracked hazel saw me as having a *history*. It sounded real, like a wooden knife whittled from a solid birch branch. I never thought of myself as having a history and would stop doing so when they dropped me off for work that afternoon. But when we walked around the lake that morning something hung behind me, something that sent me this way, something hard and edgy that would catch in my throat if I tried talking about it. They wouldn't press me and I wouldn't need to drag anything out to shrivel in the daylight. It was like love, I guess, with its abstract perfection. Actual details would only fuck things up.

At the trailhead Wyatt stood beside the Nova and stared east up where fat spongy clouds crashed into rocky peaks.

"Where again do you figure you dropped it?"

Melinda didn't even look up. "Like I said before, I was trying to get it in the water, but I don't know where it actually landed. I was headed southeast toward Montana Creek, so it's probably on the mountain side."

We followed the trail along the Herbert River until reaching the lake, where Wyatt suggested splitting up. Trails ran up both sides, so two of us would hike together. Melinda proposed she and I go one way, Wyatt the other. Wyatt agreed and my insides warmed like winter morning oatmeal.

If we'd found anything that day, the story would be done. We did not. Instead we just walked under the temperate overcast in a flat light with no shadows. We did look, though. Melinda admitted she'd wanted to hike with me for a little break from Wyatt. This summer fling was turning out to be more than she bargained on. He was a good guy, she insisted, but wasn't

89

handling this situation well. She couldn't see why he didn't just get the money from his parents. She asked if I agreed and of course I did. She wondered if I—a man with a history—could talk to him alone and plead her case. I tried several times over that afternoon and the next day, but they came at impotent and awkward moments. Wyatt saw me as a meddler and I felt sure he would've hit me if I didn't have sixty pounds on him. Still, I tried like I told Melinda I would.

We saw a few eagles overhead and what I thought was a marten scurry into the underbrush. She asked more friendly questions and I was able to tell a few tales that rubbed right up against the truth. I told how that dry dirt of Eastern Washington blew into everywhere and ground machinery to a stop or at least slowed it to a point where it didn't work right. We all just wanted out of that dirt. I talked of various harvest jobs, linking them all with some bullshit line about a love of being tied to the seasons. She smiled at the nomadic implications, but truthfully I'd slept in the same bed at my parents' house until I was twenty-seven. My time at Pendleton came with the inevitably I was sure other people felt when the kids went to dad's alma mater or took over the family business. Even coming north couldn't be called running. I just did the same thing as before, but somewhere else. I didn't know exactly what that same thing was—maybe fucking up, maybe killing time—and before I could figure it out we arrived on the far side of the lake and found Wyatt.

He also found nothing, though his pockets yielded a small joint. We all shared it and stomped off into the surrounding devil's club in weak search attempts. A light drizzle sifted down through the heavy canopy when we started back to the car. Wyatt's course up the north side had been boggy, so all three of us walked back together on the south trail.

"But we all have to look really hard, okay?"

Melinda and I agreed. We walked the whole way back silent in what an observer might have taken for concentrated searching. We'd been down this path before, though, and knew we wouldn't find anything new.

If a person wound up in a fight with Scotty Hove it probably wasn't their fault, just their turn. The younger Hove would fight a dock piling for eyeing him wrong, but he was of a stupid bent that would find him buying the same piling a drink ten minutes later. He was just predisposed to exploding and drifting lightly back to earth like cheap roadside fireworks, entertaining to watch until they went off in your hand.

Most assumed Scotty the more dangerous Hove, with his proven record in Lemon Creek, but Sam got my vote. He was quiet and smiled more easily. He laid claim to the better part of a U of A Southeast psychology degree and couldn't help looking smarter than his younger brother. He drove the Suburban, and where Scotty burst through the Drift-In's doors like a robber running the wrong way, threatening to tear off the small bell, Sam sauntered in with a grin saying he would just wait for someone to fuck up on their own.

"Got any whole milk, Roller?" Sam said. I first thought "roller" alluded to my extra pounds, but later guessed it a street title reverent of my time inside, though I'd never actually heard it inside. "You've been out the last few days."

"A few boat crews cleaned us out this week," I said. "Getting ready to head south, I guess. They restocked this morning, though."

"That two percent is for pussies. I need the thick shit for my bones." Scotty grabbed his groin and smiled my way. "I'm a growin' boy, dammit."

I smiled back. They were to meet with Wyatt tomorrow, and since I'd failed in both reconnaissance and gun acquisition, I could at least keep the brothers in a good mood.

"Aha." Sam hefted two sweating pints of whole milk and walked to the donut case. He smelled of over-rich exhaust and cologne too expensive for me to recognize.

"Tell you what," I said. "The donuts aren't suppose to go on half price till three, but because of your milk troubles I'll cut you guys the deal."

Scotty nodded and tried talking through a mouthful of his already opened milk.

"Fuck yeah." He flashed a hand signal I assumed represented our mutual history. "Membership has its privileges."

Sam just smiled and pointed to the jelly-filled.

"Gonna take more than half-priced donuts to cover for your friends' fuckup."

The muscles in my ribs jumped like a backwards cough. I put my full concentration into handling the tongs, like I was cutting wires on a bomb. Maybe I was.

"I just sell donuts, Sam."

"Sure you do," Sam said. "Sure you do. And you're a good guy and you're smart enough."

"Street smarts," Scotty added. He jammed half of his donut into his mouth and waited for Sam to pay.

"Thanks, guys. Seven twenty-nine, please."

Sam pulled a ratty ten from his front pocket. "Keep the change."

"I don't need it." A lie. Every little bit helped.

"I think you might, boss." Sam leaned against the glass countertop. It groaned but he didn't even flinch, as if broken glass didn't worry him. "I think you need all of this. This job, this place. I think you know it's better here for people with a little mud on their boots. It's good for you and you're a good man for it. Like I said, smart enough."

"People are more understanding than Outside." Scotty didn't make eye contact, perhaps still stinging from being cuffed on the ear and sent home by the world down south.

"You staying the winter?" Sam said.

I set to straightening some already straight cigarette displays. "Plan to. We'll see."

"It ain't as bad as folks make it out to be." Sam flashed a reminiscent smile. "They got open gym nights for hoops. Always someone to drink with. I don't care what people say, cabin fever at least makes us find some interesting ways to have fun. Long as you got friends, you'll make it okay."

"Sounds good."

"It's getting cold, though. Time to get friends."

"Like a squirrel's gotta gather nuts," Scotty chimed in. Sam shot a silencing glance and went on.

"Don't fuck up a winter for some summer trash that don't give a shit about the people here anymore than they do some stuffed bear they take pictures with for friends back home. It ain't worth it."

I nodded and looked down. Sam leaned in to meet my eyes.

"Once that snow starts falling, it don't matter how much money anyone's daddy's got. It just gets cold."

Scotty wiped heavy milk from the corner of his mouth and shot me another insider's grin. "I know why you're doing it, and I feel for ya. I wouldn't mind tapping that ass myself."

"I'll let Wyatt know that if he stops in."

I flushed after saying it, and might have even vomited up my breakfast of beef jerky if I didn't hear Sam's booming laugh.

Scotty stared at the floor until his big brother slugged his shoulder.

"Way to leave yourself wide open, dipshit."

Scotty laughed by default. "Yeah, fucker…"

Sam guided him through the door.

"You'll fit in just fine, man. Smart enough."

Then they were gone with a jingle of the small overhead bell, like some angel getting his wings and flying the hell out of there.

My new favorite song came on the radio just before I got the call about Wyatt. I only picked up a few new lyrics, something about having both feet on the floor and two hands on the wheel. The words made me want to get in a car and blast away. They made me wonder what I was doing in a job that would never get me a car in a town with no roads out.

I considered not answering the counter phone until the song ended to hear the DJ say the title, but Jimmy called from his office in the back.

"Phone!"

I heard Melinda crying before the receiver touched my ear. I caught only bits and pieces at first, her voice riding over sobs like a trailer on a buckboard road. I told her to calm down and asked if she was okay.

"I'm fine. But Wyatt's in bad shape."

She collected herself enough to tell me how Wyatt left to meet the Hoves that morning. He'd been dropped off at Bartlett Memorial just after one with his apartment's phone number taped to his forehead.

"They're flying him to Seattle," she said, gaining composure then losing it again. "Everyone said these guys weren't serious. I thought they would just scare him."

I guessed the Hoves must've gotten tired of hearing that, but I didn't say it. I asked where she was.

"I'm at the airport, on the charter side. The jet's leaving as soon as he gets here."

I told her I'd be there in ten minutes, hung up the phone and went to Jimmy's office. He'd at least overheard my side of the call, and most likely eavesdropped on the whole thing. Hiring ex-cons granted certain privileges. I promised it wouldn't be more than an hour, two tops.

His chair reclined with a creak. "You have been a good hand." This came as if I spent my day branding cattle instead of pushing cigarettes and fountain drinks. I reminded him I hadn't missed a shift or asked for time off in seven months. I would even come in at nine tomorrow morning, three hours early, to make it up to him. Jimmy pushed himself upright with an exhale. Walking behind the counter he said it better not become a habit. Then, softer, he told me not to get caught up in something I'd wish I hadn't. I didn't even hear the bell ring on my way out.

The ambulance passed as I neared the airport. I considered flagging them down but a stop seemed unlikely, even though I had to look like a potential customer. I couldn't remember the last time I'd run and my thick forearms glowed red in the afternoon sun. I stopped running to spit thickly on the sidewalk and settled into a brisk, breathy walk.

My shirt stuck to my back and my side ached as I paralleled the chain link fence approaching the charter services. The ambulance idled quietly though its lights still popped. The rig sat backed up to the side of a small jet. A surprising number of people obscured Wyatt's stretcher as they moved him to the plane. Melinda reached among the tubes and clipboards to rest her hand on him. At the plane's nose two pilots in flight suits watched a floatplane on approach. One pointed at the plane and both broke out in quickly-quelled laughter.

Melinda saw me entering the charter building and her eyes dashed between Wyatt and where I waited inside. Call me an asshole, but I warmed a little when she finally took off towards the office. Inside she fell into my arms, and didn't seem to care when the sweat from my shirt soaked into hers.

"It wasn't supposed to go like this." Wyatt was mostly conscious, she said, but had trouble breathing and more broken bones than Bartlett cared to count.

I pointed to the jet. "Is this really necessary?"

Melinda explained how Wyatt's parents paid for a special insurance program covering medevac flights back to the states from remote areas. They'd insisted on the policy when he spent the last winter surfing in Belize and Costa Rica. She broke down at the explanation's end.

"Do you know how damn expensive that has to be?"

I honestly had no idea. She looked over her shoulder at the stretcher and shook her head.

"All that money and his fucking pride wouldn't let him call them up."

I put my arm around her shoulder. To my surprise it felt okay and she didn't move.

"What about the police?"

Her eyes instinctively scanned the chain link fence.

"Not yet, and it'd probably be best if, y'know…"

I did know. Just because something felt inevitable was no reason to grab its leash and pull it in.

"So are you going?"

She chuckled, sending a little snot out her wet nose.

"The policy only covers family. So I'm stuck here."

I tightened my arm around her. The sun was setting and my breath returned. I actually felt benefits from my short run. My belly seemed smaller and real blood flowed through my veins.

I gave her the key to my apartment, reminding her to be careful and approach from the back, where my door wasn't visible to someone watching from Wyatt's window. I would meet her when I got off work at ten, in four hours. She agreed and I released her. I hoped for a good luck kiss but knew it wouldn't fit just yet.

I was walking back in the Drift-In when I heard the coming night's air ripped down the seams, a sound that could only be Wyatt's jet leaving us to clean up after him.

I didn't go looking for Scotty Hove that night, just like I'd never gone looking for anything in my life. I just worked my shift and spent the night considering vaguely-chivalrous acts, like lifting money out of the till or giving Melinda my coffee can for her part of the debt. I looked for the Hoves whenever the bell above the door rang, but they never came in. And maybe Scotty wasn't looking for me in the lot behind the Drift-In, which I cut through every night on my way home. Maybe he was just walking and thinking about things, maybe he too was just cutting through on his way somewhere. Maybe he was checking to see if any donuts were left. I don't know. I didn't ask.

If he hadn't been smiling, I probably wouldn't have hit him. But he was smiling, smiling with a cockiness that saved me the trouble of asking if Wyatt was their handiwork. Smiling like he'd told me so. Smiling like he would find her and I wouldn't do a damn thing about it.

I'd bought the big glass bottle of flavored iced tea because I knew Melinda liked the brand and drank it regularly with her donuts. The bottle lay cupped in my hand one second and against Scotty's greasy temple the next. It didn't shatter like the movies promised, but rather made a dopey *bonk*, stunning my hand and sending Scotty to one knee. He cursed and rose, falling toward me with a whiny growl. This time the bottle shattered. Shards dug into his scalp, and some cut back into my palm though I wouldn't realize it until blood hit my carpet ten minutes later. I grabbed the collar of his jacket and threw him to the ground, really only speeding the path he was already on. He didn't try breaking his fall, and his head bounced as high off the pavement as his limp neck allowed.

I suppose I should have issued some warning, told him and his brother not to bother Melinda or me. But I hadn't prepared a speech and my hands shook, and I doubt anything would have sunk in. Scotty just lay there. Raspberry iced tea mixed with blood in his hair and his eyes twitched like a dog dreaming about running.

Melinda noticed my bleeding hand first and, damn me to hell, I loved it. I tried downplaying the injury but it stung like the rain I'd just run through was vinegar. She wrapped my hand with an errant roll of paper towels and launched into a litany of questions with the same answer—I don't know. Was he dead? Did he coming looking for me? What about Sam? She dropped into my apartment's sole chair, left by a previous resident.

"This is all wrong."

I didn't argue and opened the hallway closet to get my duffel. Some things would be left due to the bag's limits— cassettes and the cheap boom box I bought at Goodwill, maybe a sweater or jacket.

She eyed the bag. "Have you got a plan?"

I had plenty and spewed them out on a breath that shook more with every minute. They all seemed solid back in the Drift-In's fluorescent safety, before I'd left a man—a kid, really—tremoring in a parking lot. We might jump an Alaska flight to Seattle or Anchorage to disappear, or a state ferry— slow but somehow intrinsically safe. We could fly one of the puddlejumper airlines to Haines or Skagway, rent a car and be off down the highway deep into Canada. Both feet on the floor, two hands on the wheel.

I thought having several ideas would be better than just one, but the more I stacked on only weakened the ones underneath. She shook her head at the whole sorry collection. I went to the cupboard, pulled down the coffee can and placed it harder than I'd intended on the table in front of her.

Her eyes asked *What the fuck?* I only nodded at the plastic lid.

She popped it off to look inside. Her eyes failed to open as wide as I hoped and at first my gut dropped, thinking some intruder had cleaned me out. But the whole amount was there. She nodded like a grade school teacher trying not to discourage a struggling student.

"Okay, that's maybe one walk-up fare to Seattle, or almost two to Anchorage." A little hope crept back into her face and I grabbed it like a skittish cat's tail.

"It could get us a long way on the ferry, or a car out of Skagway."

She shook her head and stood. She studied my sad little apartment and shifted her shoulders. I realized it was her first time there and I considered making some hot chocolate.

"I think the jets are the best idea." The ground under her feet was firming up. "Yes. Either north or south, I guess wherever there are seats open."

I tried to remember when the nightly rumbles through the valley woke me up.

"I hear one every morning about three," I said.

"That's the mail plane," she said. "But I think the airlines start at about six." She nodded to herself. "We'll head over first thing in the morning."

She glanced around once more with purpose, and I suddenly worried that she'd found the three-month old *Penthouse* in my bathroom cabinet.

"I don't think we should stay here."

"A hotel room," I said. "It can't be more than a hundred bucks. We can go to the new place by the airport."

"I have to get some things together." She ran a hand through her knotting hair. Her eyes snapped to meet mine. "Can you go get the room?"

"I can't leave you alone."

Her first smile of the night crooked her cheek. She grabbed my good hand.

"That's sweet, but if Sam puts things together or Scotty can talk, you're a bigger target than me. We should get you out of sight first." She squeezed my hand a little more. "I just have to grab some stuff from my place and the airport office."

It took incredible energy to let go of her hand, but little to wrap my own around the bundle in the coffee can.

"Take this with you. Just in case."

When I walked into that hotel lobby, I knew things would work out all right. The lights were bright and safe and a calm low music played. Nothing too terrible could happen while music so melancholy filled the background. I held my bandaged hand out of view though the native kid behind the counter seemed much more interested in returning to the TV at his desk than giving me the once over. I was Mr. Upton—Melinda's favorite high school teacher—and would only need the room one night. I needed a four-thirty a.m. wake up call—tonight wasn't to be trusted to alarm clocks, Melinda insisted. And my wife—I stumbled on the word it felt so good—she would be showing up just a little later. Would he be so kind as to just give her the room number and send her up?

The room itself calmed me even more, though I did stand over the clean toilet waiting to vomit the first five minutes after entering. Nothing came. My window looked out over the airport and I could sit watching for her, but she said she would be angry to find me awake when she arrived. At least one of us should be rested tomorrow. I debated over how undressed I should get, unsure of how she expected to find me in bed. I lay down fully clothed on top of the covers and within minutes the decision was made for me. If I had any dreams that night they are gone to me now.

The jet noise woke me. At first I assumed it was the mail plane making its middle of the night departure. When I saw daylight bleeding around the drapes, my gut starting dancing. The room looked the same, the entryway light still on. I tore the curtains open. A grey drizzle hung low over the airport, obscuring the now-gone jet and anything farther than a few hundred feet up Douglas Island. The clock near the bed read six forty-five. I cursed repeatedly without realizing it until a tired fist rapped against the wall behind my room's mirror. I quieted and walked in angry circles. Only as I shouldered my duffel to leave did I see the envelope wedged under the door.

I had no right to be angry with the native kid, he'd just been doing his job. My wife did indeed arrive a little later, about three a.m. She'd asked for the time of our wake-up call and then chuckled at the early hour. The clerk even attempted to imitate her laugh. *I'm not getting up that early* she'd joked with him and changed it to eight o'clock. Now he looked nervously back down the hall for her.

I smiled to relax him. "Yeah, she's the boss."

I paid up and stood there awkwardly after receiving my change. I had not stayed in many hotels and didn't know when I could leave. When he wished me a second "good day, sir" and turned to the freshly-arrived day shift girl, I figured myself free to go. I liked the hotel, though, and took a seat in an overstuffed lobby chair, facing a box of donuts. Drift-In donuts, picked up by the maintenance guy on his way to work. Unaccustomed to being the customer, I chose a greasy one I thought the other guests were least likely to miss. I pulled the envelope from my pocket and eyed its contents once more.

The $620 inside, mostly twenties and fifties, didn't leave her note a lot of room, but it was short and concise and didn't demand much space. The details were understandably vague. The money was my original sum minus what I took for the hotel room and a little traveling money she had needed. She felt bad for misleading me but it was for the best. She and the Gustavus man—apparently more than just a friend—had counted on Wyatt caving sooner and calling his parents to bail him out. And that would have been that, the end of the summer. And the Hoves? Well, they weren't supposed to be so determined or violent. All that and a lot of things that didn't come out quite right. She hoped Wyatt and the Hoves would never hear of the note's contents, and that what was left of my money would at least get me out of here and started again, maybe down south. Who knew? We might meet again and maybe she would get a chance to repay what she borrowed. I was a true and reliable soul, and she'd enjoyed talking to me that day we spent walking around Windfall Lake, searching lazily for something that was never there in the first place.

I pocketed the money and out of the clerk's view tore the note into tiny pieces. I downed another donut slowly, interspersed with parts of the note. It was delicious.

Jimmy was all smiles when I walked into the Drift-In thirty minutes early. I purposely avoided the short cut behind the building, but when I peeked back there it looked as pure and innocent as every day before.

"Thought I'd spell you a little early," I said. "For covering for me yesterday."

He set to work cleaning up and didn't inquire about my injury, just saying I should change the bandage and handle any food with my other hand. I promised I would. He gave me a quick passdown and was out the door at quarter to nine. He walked away with the stride of a man who owned a little more of the day than he planned or maybe deserved. Whatever he did with that time—set the world on fire, fuck things up, or just waste it like he always did—it belonged to him.

I was changing my bandages, my back to the door, when the bell above the door announced the first customer of my shift. I had the radio turned up a little louder than Jimmy liked and if my new favorite song came on, I would listen carefully to find out who sang it, maybe even call the station if they didn't say. Then I might just hop over to the Nugget Mall and buy the album if the music store had it. Then I could listen and listen to that song until I knew every damn word by heart.

AURORA'S STORIES

Aurora has stories, but you will probably never hear them. Aurora lives in the small northern town she was born in thirty-four years ago. Barring any unforseen circumstances, she will continue living there and most likely die there peacefully someday. Though she never thinks of her own demise, this would be fine with her.

Aurora lives with her father in a house he bought forty-one years ago. Every once in a while and for no apparent reason, he states how it is not the newest or fanciest house in town, but is paid for and he sees no reason to move. Aurora can only agree. The house has been home her entire life, except for the summer she was twenty-four and got that little apartment above a restaurant downtown. It was fun but her dad soon complained about his back hurting him again. He needed her help for a little while, so she moved back in and hasn't left yet. Aurora has slept in the same bed most every night she can remember, save for the time in her apartment, a few trips down south and some long-ago sleepovers. Her dad claims she needs a new mattress, but Aurora isn't sure. It is still comfortable and she doesn't understand how a bed could wear out. She doesn't move much at night and never has trouble sleeping.

Aurora's mom used to live with them, but when Aurora was small her mom got sick twice and died. The first time Aurora's mom got sick she got better but only after they all took a trip down south. Her mom had been weak for a few months, so they got on the state ferry and rode it into Seattle's harbor. Back then the boats docked right downtown. Aurora looked up at the shiny buildings and felt her mom getting better already. She asked her dad to buy the Space Needle and he said he would see what he could do but her mom's health came first. They stayed at a relative's house close to stores and restaurants, and the sun shined everyday. Her mom went to the hospital for a while until one day she came back better. The next day they got on the ferry and sailed away. Aurora cried watching the Space Needle disappear in the rain behind the boat. Her dad told her the people of Seattle would miss the needle too much, and it would never fit in her little town.

"I guess I see what you mean," Aurora said.

The second time Aurora's mom got sick even Seattle could not save her and Aurora didn't get to go. Her parents flew out to Juneau early one morning and left the neighbor lady who smelled like old furniture to watch Aurora. The lady never knew what to say to her, and Aurora felt sorry for her. One day the phone rang and made the lady sit down and cry. The lady didn't need to say anything then. Aurora's dad came home a few days later and they buried her mom up on the hill with all the other people from town. Her dad brought Aurora back a little model of the Space Needle. She told her dad she put it somewhere special but she really just walked to the bridge and let the model drop into the river. She felt bad the next day and walked up and down the riverbed, but never found her Space Needle. She hasn't been to Seattle since, but misses the big city sometimes. Now the Alaska ferries only go as far south as Bellingham. You can take a bus up to Vancouver, B.C. in an hour and it is cleaner and prettier and with the exchange rate things works out real well.

Aurora really kissed a boy when she was fifteen. She kissed a few boys before then and has kissed a couple since, but that was a real kiss. It happened on the rocks overlooking the bay, down a short trail everyone in town knows about but rarely walks down. He was fifteen also, and always got in trouble at school for saying funny things. Sometimes no one laughed when he said things, but Aurora always smiled, even when she didn't understand what he meant. They would walk out to the rocks sometimes and talk about nothing in particular. He would help her up the steeper slopes and often held her hand even after she no longer needed help. One evening he told her about his dad's new job way up in Cordova and then he kissed her. She didn't know whether to be happy or sad, so she chose happy and kissed him back. It was like how they kiss on TV.

Since then a few other boys have kissed Aurora and done a little more. She never really cared for it but they seemed to enjoy themselves so she let them. Ten years ago she heard how that boy from the rocks fell off a crab boat up north in the Bering Strait. For a long time she thought about him in that cold water, drowning despite the fact he always claimed to be a good swimmer. Later she thought of him somehow finding his way ashore and walking back to her town, or maybe to someplace over in Russia. Aurora knew it was up there somewhere and saw him making the Russian girls laugh and smile even though they couldn't understand a thing he said. Aurora used to think of the boy in a lot of ways, but now she just thinks of him on the rocks that day they were both fifteen.

Aurora works at the post office and enjoys it. She took the job eleven years ago, after working many summers in various jobs at local gift shops and restaurants. Her dad told her if she planned on staying she had best get something with benefits and retirement. Aurora agreed but couldn't think about retiring and rarely felt sick. On the rare times she calls in sick she feels so guilty she doesn't pick up her own mail until she gets better. Aurora likes wearing the uniform and talking to the people who drop off the big mailbags in the morning and pick them up in the afternoon. Occasionally the pilots who fly the mail up in their little planes help them with the bags, and on rainy and snowy days they joke with Aurora how people better enjoy their mail for all their hard work. Sometimes Aurora hears their voices shake a little.

The summers are busier for the post office with customers off all the cruise ships trying to mail boxes back to wherever in the world they came from. Most are friendly, but some get mad and many are confused with postal rates or whether or not Alaska is a state and similar things. They make Aurora laugh to herself, but only after they have gone out the door. She likes winters better. Winter means light loads, short lines and all local customers. They are nice and rarely in a hurry. The postmaster lets Aurora and the others listen to the radio while they work and it helps pass the time. The A.M. station from the city is hard to get and plays too many sports for Aurora. The only station they get clearly comes from the next town over the hills. She likes to think how those people are talking just over the mountains and she can hear them, even if she doesn't always like the music they play. Her favorite part is the Listener Bulletin Board every five minutes after the hour. Listeners leave messages for people they can't find, which the DJ reads in hopes that the other person is also listening. *Joe Coskins—I borrowed the chainsaw from your shed and will be done with it tomorrow. Come by if you need it sooner—Stuart.* Things like that. Often Aurora doesn't know the people from the other town, but occasionally she hears a name she recognizes. Once there was a message for a man named Terry that his friend went to Juneau and would be back in two days. Terry came in to check his mail and Aurora asked if he heard the message on the radio. Terry had not and thanked her several times and Aurora felt good about it. Most everybody thanks Aurora, even when she knows they are angry about postal rates going up or a box costing more to mail than they thought or getting envelopes they don't want. Aurora appreciates this and if it were up to her she would never put bills or final notices in their mailboxes. She would only hand out fat envelopes with happy handwriting on them and boxes from old friends and flyers offering twenty percent off something they really wanted. She would send their biggest boxes wherever they needed to go really fast and for free.

Aurora studied hard for her driver's license when she turned sixteen and passed the test on the first try. Still, she doesn't drive much. She doesn't own a car and only drives her dad's truck on the rare occasion he goes downtown and ends up in no shape to drive home. The post office is only five blocks from her house and she can walk on even the coldest winter day. She mostly rides her bike. She has always liked bikes and at one time could ride one very fast. In the third grade she got her first bike—a boy's bike, a BMX racer. She had picked a different one out of the Sears catalog, but when her dad filled out the order form he must have put a wrong number in somewhere. A month later a box arrived full of parts that assembled into a boy's bike.

"I can break it down and send the box of parts back for an exchange if you want," her dad said, but he didn't sound he wanted to, and it being spring all the kids already had their bikes out.

"It's okay, dad," Aurora said. "No one will notice."

Some kids made fun of her at first but they got bored

and stopped soon after. Aurora found the bike fit her—she was never built entirely like a girl anyway—and she rode everywhere. Mostly she rode alone, but when she rode with others she found it didn't take much effort to pull out in front. She knew it rude to pull away if someone was willing to ride with her, but also realized she was fast on that bike.

The last day of school each year was Events Day, where everyone competed in different contests—running, obstacle courses and all kinds of things. Aurora usually just watched, curious as to who could run the fastest or jump the farthest. She knew it wasn't her and had never entered anything before. That year the last event was a K-6th bike race, though, so she signed up. There was supposed to be a separate boys and girls race, but the only girls who signed up were Aurora and a sixth grader with a real girl's bike. They were told to race with the boys because the day was getting late and the teachers were tired. Also entered in the race was a fifth grade boy who won everything. He'd always won things in the past, he'd won a lot already that day, and Aurora would watch him go on to win many things for years to come. The race ran from the school through downtown and back up the river trail. If Aurora could stay near the boy until the river, that would be good enough for her. When the race started she pulled out ahead and never saw any of them the rest of the way. She was scared to look over her shoulder so she just kept pedaling. People at the finish line looked surprised when Aurora rode out of the trees by the river and across the dodgeball courts to win. They clapped and yelled her name but still appeared confused. The boy who won everything finished close behind her and they all cheered loudly. Aurora figured they cheered better for him because they had more practice doing it. He skidded to a stop and looked tired and angry. He said things about his chain slipping and being tired from winning everything else on Events Day, and everyone agreed. Over the summer he forgot to stay angry and talked to Aurora sometimes, but Aurora always thought he never forgot to be confused and sad about the race. She finally asked her dad to trade her bike in for a girl's bike. He said it was too late for an exchange but he loved her and took care of her even when he didn't want to, so he finally found someone to trade with. Her girl's bike was prettier, more comfortable, and pump as hard as she might, Aurora could never make it go fast. She just rode around town no faster or slower than anyone else. The boy who won everything grew up and eventually stopped winning. He became a little nicer as a result and calls back to Aurora whenever he picks up his mail. Aurora hasn't seen him ride a bike in a very long time.

Aurora can keep a secret. Not many people tell her secrets, but when she gets one she guards it like gold or a stray kitten. Like most people she forgets many secrets eventually, but she remembers a big one. One night in a long-gone January when the wind was howling, she needed some female things from the store. Her dad insisted she take his truck. On the way home she saw a girl walking who had been two grades behind Aurora in school. They had never really talked before but knew each other in a way natural to everyone in her town. The girl looked cold and drunk. Aurora knew she lived outside town and had almost a mile of walking ahead. Aurora pulled over, hiding her female things under the seat.

"Can I give you a ride?" Aurora said.

The girl smiled and said Aurora's name in a warm way she rarely heard. She got in and they drove. The girl was in fact drunk—she admitted this immediately—and mad as hell at her husband. Aurora knew her husband from school also. They both had always been nice-looking, but the girl got prettier and her husband got more handsome when they walked together, at least back then. They had spent that afternoon in the bar and ended up arguing about something. So he drove the car home and left her to walk. When they got near the girl's house, she asked Aurora if they could drive a few minutes more. So she could both warm up and cool down, the girl said, and then laughed.

"I guess it would be okay," Aurora said. Her dad was watching his favorite program for the next hour and she didn't get to drive often. They drove through town once more while the girl talked bad about her husband. Aurora didn't say so but thought it sad—in high school they seemed very much in love and now even had a little boy to prove it. After a deep breath the girl asked if Aurora could keep a secret and before Aurora could answer the girl told Aurora her husband was not the boy's father. It was another man with real nice eyes who worked on the state ferry. The girl cried and said she had never told anyone. Aurora said it was okay but didn't know what to say next, so she just said it was okay again. Then the girl wanted to go home right then, so Aurora drove her home. She got out and ran across the ice to her front door, slipping only once.

The next day the girl came to Aurora's house. She was

sober and didn't want to come in and just stayed on the porch. She thanked Aurora for the ride and asked her to please keep her secret. To this day Aurora has told no one. Aurora thinks about this secret when the man from the state ferry comes into the post office with those eyes, and when she sees the girl on the street and she smiles in a way that always says "thank you" a little. She thought about it last month when the girl's husband came in to mail some bills. He was smiling and had the boy with him. The boy is bigger now, in the fourth grade, and has nice eyes.

"You look more like your dad every year," Aurora told him. Aurora knows people will talk, but they won't hear anything from her. She hopes the boy will know what to do with those eyes.

Aurora keeps herself busy. During the summers she walks the trails outside town. She has walked them for years, but still loves each and every one of them. During the winters she goes to the high school to watch the sports teams with her dad, who yells the same things he has her whole life. *Get your hands up!* for basketball, *Suck it up!* for wrestling. She listens to music, though nothing new. Her favorite band hasn't released an album in years, but she heard they still play smaller clubs and state fairs down south. Aurora remembers when they were really popular she saw a picture of them playing a place as big as the Kingdome. There must've been ten thousand people there all yelling. Aurora couldn't see herself as one of them. They were just a lot of other people. Now that they are playing smaller places, Aurora might be able to get in.

Aurora watches a lot of TV with her dad. They watch pretty much what everyone else watches. The shows they like usually stay on a long while and the ones they don't like get cancelled most of the time. Her dad used to warn her against watching too much TV, but now they watch about the same amount and he doesn't worry anymore. Aurora figures she will know when she's watched too much TV, and she will just get up and turn the set off. People tell her she needs a computer—she would have fun with one. She works with computers at the post office and finds them helpful but not fun. She has seen the internet a few times but isn't interested. *But all that information at your fingertips*, people say. Aurora smiles and nods but doesn't want to offend people by saying she doesn't need or want all that information right now. She went to high school and can find information if she needs to, and sometimes it's more fun to find things out slowly.

Aurora has these stories and a few more, but most people will never hear them.

NAUTICAL DISASTERS

Years ago, a time now a decade gone, Mark Holder envied the deckhands on the state ferries. Back then he rode the boats to other towns as a high school athlete for wrestling tournaments or cross-country meets. He watched from the comfort of the observation lounge chairs as the guys on the icy decks tied lines and ran winches in the union-mandated warmth of snowmobile suits. On the car deck he saw haggard bosun joes guiding cars and foot traffic alike with smoke-wrinkled paws. In a land with no roads, keeping the big boats moving struck Mark as the role of blue-collar knights. At seventeen he assumed everyone over legal drinking age did what they did by their own choice.

Now he sat in the forward lounge of the M.V. *Taku* watching Juneau's Auke Bay ferry terminal drift toward the bow. The February morning outside was a mixture of off-white and pink. No races, wrestling matches or ball games waited in the dirty snow on shore. The deckhands reluctantly took their places like extras in a production about a character they'd never get to play. State bennies sure, but low seniority and freezing their asses off.

"Poor saps," Mark muttered. He set to collecting his things, a ritual that accompanied the first sighting of the destination dock. In high school this meant cramming his sleeping bag and Walkman and tapes into his duffel. When he traveled with Layla and the boy, it meant strollers, car seats, and a bottomless bag of Technicolor baby paraphernalia. This morning he traveled light—a jacket, the clothes on his back, a Stihl cap and his wallet with $8,102 inside. Mark had checked the cash no fewer than a hundred times since boarding in Haines, but now realized the hat was gone. Most likely he forgot it in the TV lounge or the bar, where the bartender had requested he leave as they passed Eldred Rock lighthouse. He hadn't planned on drinking so much, but they'd been delayed an hour and a half leaving Haines and the strong south winds didn't help. He accepted the cap as a loss. A new life deserved a new hat.

Mark made his way down to the car deck with no hurry. He would disembark after the initial rush, minimizing the chance of bumping into anyone he knew. He could easily small talk his way through an encounter—he was in Juneau for the doctor or dentist or a trip to Costco—but preferred not to. He was sobering but held his own reins tenuously. If he saw Likan working the deck, though, who knew what would happen. Mark hadn't seen him anywhere on board in the last six hours—and he'd been looking—so a peaceful off-loading appeared likely.

Mark strode up the ramp's icy grates with the second wave of auto traffic, mainly bulky campers and container trucks. The air churned his breath to dirty silver clouds and shivers ran through him without remorse. At the top of the ramp he turned to eye the *Taku*. He was giving a last look for Likan, but wouldn't admit it even if someone held his head under the cold water.

"The fuckin' blue canoe." He offered the boat a sloppy left-handed salute that looked neither nautical nor reverent. "I'll be seeing you around. Or maybe not."

A Lynden Transport truck roared past. The driver appeared split between flipping the bird or just running him over. Mark had considered riding the boat all the way south to Bellingham, but decided instead on the two-hour flight to Seattle. He didn't so much fear the two days of reflection the boat promised as he did spending another minute on a craft whose bar banished him after only three hours.

A few cabs lurked outside the terminal doors, the fenders clumped with rocky ice and their drivers smoking against their mounts. When Mark approached, a sinewy fellow in Wranglers went to put out his cigarette.

"Don't do it on my account," Mark said.

The man nodded thanks and motioned to a maroon station wagon. Mark swore he'd ridden in the same car a decade before, when the car was only twelve years old, perhaps with the same driver. The cabbie whipped them onto the freshly plowed Glacier Highway and fell in with the procession from the boat.

"People here don't know how to drive in snow," the driver said, trailing a nervous laugh.

"I hear that everywhere I've ever been," Mark said, though he'd been few places. "You'd think people here could do it."

"Yeah." Again came the cabby's nervous laugh. "Damn Outsiders is what it is. Still, you're right—there's gotta be somewhere people actually know how to drive in snow."

The driver turned up the classic rock radio station. He didn't like his small talk put to such scrutiny, and also approved greatly of the Molly Hatchet song just starting.

"Well, wherever that is," Mark said, "I ain't going there."

He watched the road roll by, remembering how the cross-country coach would make the team suit up and run from the ferry terminal to Auke Lake and back whenever the boat had a long layover here. They all bitched to high heaven, but knew Coach was right and it was for the best.

"Yeah?" The stringy driver said. "Where you off to?"

"Don't know yet." Mark loved how the words sounded, coming out on breath he could see. "South to Seattle, then somewhere warm."

"Hell, yeah. That's my plan, too."

This didn't reassure Mark. He took solace that he sat on at least four months' salary for the driver.

"Good luck to you," Mark said.

"You too, brother." The driver eased past a gravel truck. "You just save me a spot on that beach."

The computers at the ticket counter had been down for an hour. This brought the airline, or at least their polyester-clad representative behind the counter, to a relative standstill. The agent reminded Mark of an old-time schoolmarm, and eyed him as if she might hold him back another year.

"Can't I still just buy a ticket?" Mark again palmed the comfortable thickness of his wallet.

The Schoolmarm shrugged. "I don't know the walk-up fare and can't print out anything without the computer."

She saw this didn't satisfy Mark. She exhaled and looked at the clock. It read 8:39.

"There's lots of room on the eleven-fifty. If the guys can get this fixed in a hour, that's still plenty of time to get you taken care of."

"So back at nine-forty?"

"Make it ten."

"Damn computers, huh?" Mark offered this with a lazy camaraderie, but the agent eyed him warily. He worried he smelled of something he shouldn't.

"Okay, then. Ten o'clock," he said and walked away. After a few feet he turned to send a smile back over his shoulder, but the Schoolmarm had lost interest.

Outside it wasn't snowing yet, but the clouds held aspirations. He decided on a walk to the nearby Nugget Mall for an Orange Julius and a new hat. Mark reminded himself to be careful. He'd heard how since that World Trade Center thing airlines were on the lookout for suspicious customers. He would attract enough attention when he paid cash for a walkup fare. He must watch himself from here on.

Mark found the Orange Julius replaced by a vendor for some deep-fried delicacy he knew himself to be mispronouncing. The mall felt much smaller than a decade ago, and half the spaces now held pulltab shops. He went into a clothing store, considering a purchase. He imagined himself walking off the plane somewhere tropical in his present dirty jeans and hickory shirt, sweating his ass off as the new laughing stock for the locals. Being February, the store held only Helly Hansen and Cabela's work gear. The only available headwear minimized exposed skin and repelled wind, rain and snow. Sunburn was not a concern. Maybe wherever he landed would have an airport store selling flowery shirts and surfer shorts. He smiled at the thought of jamming his dirty work clothes into a bathroom garbage bin and walking out into laughing sunlight.

While looking over some energy bars, Mark caught sight of a chubby little fellow trying on windbreakers. His wife held court on each style from a nearby chair. Her verdicts were strict and unfavorable. It took several stolen glances for Mark to place him. He was from Hoonah and Mark had wrestled him in the 145-lb class three presidential elections ago. He remembered the kid as strong—Mark barely won by a point. Something had happened and here the guy stood, henpecked and trying to squeeze into a smaller man's jacket. The guy would be lucky to get a good reversal for two points on his substantial old lady. Given two weeks and a sauna suit, Mark could be back to weight and giving any senior a run for his money.

He stopped for a large breakfast soda at a snack counter. The wall clock read 9:35. This meant 10:35 up in Whitehorse, where Layla and the whole gang were packing up and getting ready for the six-hour drive back to Haines. Add in a lunch stop and it would be almost five o'clock before she walked into the empty house. None of his clothes would be missing, but the truck wasn't in the driveway. The machine would blink with her messages from last night. A day or so later the rumor being circulated by the bank tellers would reach her, how Mark took half their savings out Friday afternoon, mumbling something about investments. The amount in his wallet was admittedly a little more than half of the original $14,230, but it took a grand just to get started somewhere. Layla would eventually find his truck at the ferry terminal parking lot, and she could sell it for $1500 easy.

For the evening, though, she would just assume he was on a local bender or an impromptu drive up the highway. Mark could see her looking around the house with that mouth-breathing stare. *Mark? You here?* Mark hated that bovine stare with everything in him. That stare didn't just wonder—it had no idea where to even start wondering. The look started as an anomaly when they first started screwing around four years ago, but now showed up with the annoying regularity of a cold sore. He feared the boy was picking it up, as much as an eighteen-month old could assume such a characteristic.

The boy. Mark had avoided thinking about him until now, but that little bugger seemed to stare right at him as Mark sipped his Pepsi outside the hobby shop. In the end this whole thing would be best for him. Mark was fond of the little fellow for sure, as fond as a guy could get when he didn't know anything definite. All he asked—all he'd ever asked the last two years—was for one of those DNA tests, just to know one way or another. Then he might be willing to make the trip to Zales and make things official. Layla refused each time.

"It'll make me feel like a guest on Jerry Springer," she would say.

Mark argued that just being asked to take one at least qualified her for Maury Povich, or maybe Montel before he got sick and straightened up. No, Layla said, the boy didn't need any more drama. So Mark thought it best to leave. He'd left before, usually only getting to about 40 Mile on the highway. The farthest had been an all-day affair to Haines Junction, which he explained away as a visit to his parents who moved up there to retire, though he neglected to see them. There was no getting around this one, though. To buy some getaway time, he'd taken advantage of Layla's two-day trip with the boy and some friends up to Takhini Hot Springs outside Whitehorse. Mark realized his actions weren't very chivalrous, but as he was robbing the boy of a father figure and sporadic financial support, he felt it kept with the mood of the weekend. Everyone would hate him anyway, he might as well help them along.

Mark finished his big soda and took a last leisurely stroll over the mall's length. Sugar replaced the beer in his blood and he felt invigorated, though a cleansing vomit might still be in order. The trail back to the airport offered some privacy, so he headed out into the cold. A light snow fell and he flushed with a fear the jets would be unable to get in. He hoped for the ceilings to hold for a little longer. *Just give me that, Lord,* he thought toward the white sky, *and I won't ask for more. At least not for a while.*

The deal with Likan was this—Mark didn't hate the guy. He'd known Likan most of his life but with only a passing knowledge of the man himself, like a relative seen at holiday dinners. But Likan had been given a golden opportunity, held the brass ring in his hand, and let go of his own volition. As a representative of the many who would never see such a break, Mark felt obligated to smack the guy upon sight, at least one solid shot to the gut.

Until the previous winter, Mark simply knew the man eight years his senior as a ferry worker. He heard a few stories of Likan's high school hi-jinks and waved when they were the only two cars passing on the street, but otherwise only saw him working the boats on sports trips. Like too many guys, Likan long ago fell for the first girl to open her pearly gates on some cold Saturday night and soon found himself with little more than a moody roommate who lived in sweats and named their kids after her favorite television characters. A true seaman, he accepted these onshore consequences silently, dragging them around like a bum leg injured in a stupid childhood stunt.

Then, a year and a half ago, Likan disappeared. Not in some cowardly or irresponsible way, but a damn near heroic tragedy. He regularly worked the *Kennicott* runs down to Bellingham—if a person knew his old lady they saw why he opted for the long hauls. Taking advantage of a lengthy layover, the boat's crew set to some cleaning and testing of the emergency equipment. They lowered Likan and several others down in the orange and white lifeboats, one man to a boat, to put the little crafts through their paces. From there, several stories sprung. One said a yell and splash were heard, another said simply a splash. In the most common version searchers found the boat idling west of the docks, empty save for the bulky life preserver the workers were required to take but never wore. Bellingham's finest and the Coast Guard swept the harbor for two days while the *Kennicott* sailed north minus one.

The wife and little Likans enjoyed a month as Haines' charity darlings, the benefactor of school food drives, Elks fundraisers and Cub Scout raffles. Those who knew his wife threw around the word suicide, but Likan owned his share of hunting rifles and wouldn't leave a boat shorthanded in mid-sailing. He would've done it with more tact or at least chosen the colder waters of his home harbor to expedite the process. Likan was just unlucky and fell in. End of story.

Approaching the terminal Mark heard the roar of a jet through the snow and clouds. He warmed and reached back to check his wallet once more, resting fat right where he wanted it. A small line extended back from the airline counter and a bony blonde worked alongside the Schoolmarm. The computers were up and running. Mark thought he saw a familiar coat in line, though, and ducked into the gift store to feign interest in a few cartoonish sweaters until the line thinned.

Mark didn't know exactly how to act when the blonde agent quoted him the walkup fare. If he acted too surprised, paying in cash would look odd. Taking the price without comment might also send up a red flag. He already felt the Schoolmarm's sidelong glances from the computer to his left.

"Ain't exactly givin' them away, huh?" Mark laughed.

The blonde shrugged. "Pays to plan ahead."

Mark pulled six one-hundred-dollar bills from his wallet and slid them across the counter with his best reluctant smile.

"Any bags to check, sir?"

"No, ma'am," Mark said and took back his change. The Schoolmarm's eyes looked hard at her screen and her typing sped up, even though her station stood empty.

Mark kept his hands busy at the security gate so the agents wouldn't see them shake. He shucked his jacket and steel-toed Wolverines and emptied his pockets into the little dishes.

"You can't take this on board."

A hairy man in a tight sweater with a fabric badge sown on held up Mark's Leatherman. Mark flushed, but the big man simply handed the tool back.

"If you want, you can run down to the gift shop and get an envelope and a couple bucks worth of stamps and mail it to yourself."

Mark looked around. A similarly-uniformed girl sat wide-eyed watching his boots and jacket on a monitor glowing with crazy colors.

"Why don't you just keep it, man?" Mark said.

"I've already got seven this month alone. I sell them on eBay." The sweatered bear looked at the clock. "You've got an hour before your flight boards. Why not save yourself fifty bucks? Be stupid to do otherwise."

Mark took the Leatherman back and shoved it deep in his pocket. All those tightened screws and opened bottles weren't worth this.

"Can I leave my stuff here for a minute?"

The Grizzly nodded. It would all be waiting for his return. He felt for the wallet once more and took off down the carpet, feeling childlike in his socks.

Likan came back to life three months after drowning in Bellingham harbor, though it wasn't exactly the angels rolling away the stone. He showed up drunk on the doorstep of a former Haines High schoolmate now living in Everett. The friend kept in good enough contact with folks back home to know the man on his step was dead. The two shared an understandably awkward breakfast at a nearby Denny's.

Two days later Likan was back in Haines with plans of

returning to the ferries. He took the welcomes home with wild-eyed detachment and a smile. He spoke little. Stories trailed behind him like a silly cape he thought he'd removed. The one that stuck claimed he'd suffered some sort of traumatizing amnesia in his tumble from the boat. He fumbled his way to shore and, despite not remembering his hometown and wife and kids, managed to fashion a new life in north Seattle. He took a basement apartment, worked simple labor for temp agencies, and began spelling his last name Lykin. Then one rainy night everything came back and he drank his way to that Everett doorstep.

Likan's wife bought the story, though Mark was confident she smacked him hard with her thick paw when she thought hard about it. The state ferry system assigned him light duty at the local terminal and put him through some psych evals in Juneau to determine his seaworthiness. Finally they let him back on the decks and even allowed his odd family to keep what they'd already received in his death settlement. The family quietly retook the routine of going to the store, school pageants and home basketball games.

Still, Mark heard stories and harbored his own doubts. Amnesia? Even the soap opera hacks abandoned that crap years ago. Word was Likan bid the Bellingham run for months prior, planning the whole thing and stashing a little money each trip in a Greyhound station locker in the nearby Fairhaven district. The slightly misspelled name was a guise enabling him to still cash checks and use his Alaska ID. All this was conjecture born at the Fogcutter, but Mark knew it to be true.

That was why Likan had something coming. Looking at his own sloppy affair, Mark would kill for the seamless lines of Likan's caper. Although Likan never did wrong by him, Mark had to wallop the man on sight. Likan would take the hit, and just look up with eyes acknowledging it was nothing personal.

A young couple dropped into the chairs behind Mark after he'd spent five minutes sitting there with his pen and envelope. Despite Mark's proximity, they soon set upon each other like drugged mud wrestlers.

Where to send the Leatherman? Sending the tool home didn't make sense and seemed, even to Mark, a cruel gesture. Layla wouldn't need it, and without a father figure she would have the boy behind knitting needles rather than tools by the time he turned five. She might also take this as a sign of his ultimate return. He considered mailing it to his folks up in Haines Junction, but didn't know if the postage was adequate for Canada. They initially wouldn't want the reminder of their disappointing son, but would also keep the tool in hopes of his return. He thought of Jim Huffsy, whose portable CD player he borrowed last fall and dropped in the river while fishing. Maybe he could just write "MARK HOLDER, SOMEWHERE SUNNY." He dreamed of walking off the plane to some thatch hut post office and finding the Leatherman waiting. He would spend days on the beach drinking from coconuts and telling the wild tale to lotion-covered co-eds on spring break who would find the story oddly erotic.

He put the pen to paper, but just then the row of interconnected seats shifted with a jolt. The girl had taken things up a notch and now straddled her boyfriend's lap. The jump sent a single blue line across Mark's envelope. She held her boyfriend's face in her hands and tears welled in her shut eyes. Even bundled for the cold, her white hip meat peeked suggestively over her jeans. She bore an innocent softness but moved with a whimpering warmth gleaned from music videos and late night cable TV. She slipped her arms inside his Juneau-Douglas letterman's jacket and seemed to shrink into the fabric. The jacket's shoulder bore a year that Mark never thought would come but was now six weeks gone. The guy just laid back and took it like the fellows in dirty movies, wiping off the errant tears hitting his cheek with equal parts annoyance and enjoyment. Truly the breakfast of champions. A big duffel beside his seat said he'd given post-graduation Juneau a chance and things hadn't worked out. The girl's fervor suggested she wasn't yet free to follow and knew her pale soft form would be lost when he walked off the plane into the throng of beautiful people that everyone up here assumed waited down in Sea-Tac.

Mark stood and walked to an adjacent mail drop box. He used the flat top to write "Tommy Likan, General Delivery, Haines, Alaska," on the envelope. He put the Leatherman in, sealed the envelope and dropped it in. He sent the pen after for good measure. Wandering back to security, Mark studied the letterman's jacket and the writhing girl. Football, basketball, and one emblem he assumed was track. The kid looked big but dumb and slow. Probably a linebacker, a bench-warming bruiser, and a shot-putter, respectively. The speed and quickness of the Outside would drop him like a pool cue to his kneecaps. The kids stopped making out when they noticed Mark watching them. The girl wiped her eyes.

"What are you looking at?"

Mark could make Layla buy the whole damn thing. It wouldn't be easy but this was a girl who watched *Matlock* to the final credits to see whodunit. Mark could come up with something—nothing as dumbass as amnesia—and work his way back in. This knowledge shook him enough to rattle his change and make his bowels groan. Everyone needed someone who bought their bullshit but wanted someone who didn't.

Still, going back was no option. He would find himself sitting in the bleachers at home games, saying hello to passersby and exchanging small talk. He would never hear their talk about his ferry trip and large withdrawal and subsequent redeposit three days later. The rumors would rattle around him like kids playing unseen under the bleachers. He would sit there in a fat dumb oblivion with the world roaring around him, maybe sharing popcorn and bleacher space with the Likans and their sticky-fingered litter. Layla and Momma Likan would chomp on candy sold by the senior class and complain how that Atkins diet was impossible to stick to and dangerous to boot. Mark and Likan could talk about Haines' lack of a shooting guard and small forward and how this winter was cold like the winters used to be and the possibilities of Likan getting Mark a cushy year-round gig at the ferry terminal. Mark couldn't punch Likan. He'd lost the right. Everyone in that gym would look at them and think that there sat the two biggest dipshits in the northern Lynn Canal.

Mark couldn't do that. He couldn't control everything, but he wouldn't do himself in.

The kids wouldn't make it. Mark did his best to assure them he wasn't saying this to be an asshole, but to help them. Young local love was tenuous enough alone. Throw in some distance—and up here the only distance was long—and the pleasures down south offered, and it was best to just call things off right now and save yourself some big phone bills. Maybe just knock out a quick last one in the car with the heater on high. But wear a rubber or pull out, Mark warned the kid. That girl's hips, all plush and singing like they did in those low-rise jeans, had few options. They would either explode at their first chance with children or chocolate, or start swinging around to see how the local leftovers measured up to her letterman hero.

Mark knew he was no wordsmith, but felt his aim was true. He expected his honesty—at ten-thirty a.m. and twenty-eight degrees outside—to hit them like a bland but ultimately filling bowl of oatmeal. He was surprised when the kid rose and then kept rising. The girl wrapped around his big thigh and wiped her eyes against his jeans.

"Fuck you," she said.

Mark nodded to her point. "I know it ain't what you want to hear, but I just wish somebody had…"

The kid stripped off his letterman's jacket and dropped it on the girl. She could've used it as a shelter. Like everyone who grew up in the neighboring small towns, Mark always heard the fast kids from Juneau took speed and the big ones took steroids.

The kid's gaze dropped. "Where the hell are your shoes, dumbass?"

Mark pointed toward the security gate.

"Over there, but that isn't important." Mark felt suddenly naked with only a layer of wool between his toes and the brute.

"He smells like shit," the girl called from beneath the jacket.

"I bet I'm fresher than you'll be on Sunday mornings next month, honey."

A tremor ran from the giant kid's legs, through the floor and into Mark's socks.

"You little shit…"

"Easy there, Kong." Mark dropped his stance, lowering his center of gravity. He thought of David and Goliath, the lone Bible story he didn't find overly preachy. He didn't have the slingshot or numchucks or whatever, but David didn't have four years of varsity wrestling and a knack for single-leg takedowns. "If you're heading south, you better learn who not to screw with."

"And you're gonna learn to keep your mouth shut."

The kid advanced, dimming the lights behind his shoulders. Mark curled his toes against the tight carpet and loosed a big breath. Something was going to happen and he welcomed the certainty. This whole trip had been too goddamn wishy-washy up to now.

Mark waited for the kid to get close enough and slid forward onto his left knee. He drove his shoulder into the kid's thigh, embracing the leg and firing himself skyward. The leg smashed into his collarbone and stayed true as a power pole. A quick ballpark estimate told Mark the kid had fifty pounds on him. After this hurried math, things moved along with a welcome speed. For a big fellow the kid had quickness—maybe he took speed *and* steroids. Mark felt big hands on his side and the world slip away from his socks. He caught glimpses of the ceiling lights and a few advertisements on the walls—a helicopter company, the Westmark hotels throughout the state, and a pro-life ad with a cherubic baby. He heard the girl yell "Terry!" and Mark repeated the name, pleading but still manly. He swung his arms and legs out to give the impression of an honest fight. Only his left foot made contact, smacking one of the metal chair arms on what could only be the way down.

He hit the carpet square on his back, his thinly covered heels cracking the floor sharply. His breath rushed out and bile rose in his throat. He attempted sitting up but only made it to one elbow. The girl had pulled her beast into the corner. The kid panted and muttered curse words to himself.

"Own good...can't see..." Mark could only sputter on his limited breath. He looked toward the security gates, suddenly very worried about his jacket, his Wolverines, and his loose change.

The Schoolmarm was preparing to pass through security, but stopped and now talked with the Grizzly agent. She held an important clipboard in one hand and a small radio in the other. Never losing sight of Mark, she exchanged a few words with the security agent. He nodded and took up his own radio from a nearby table. They both started talking into their radios, maybe just to each other, but most likely to someone who sat waiting for this type of thing. Mark laid back and waited for his breath to return. Things were out of his hands now.

GOATS

This would be their first winter Outside in six years. With all that had happened, everyone agreed it would do Lilly and Tom good. On September twenty-ninth they packed a duffel each and loaded them in the truck with Ignatius, their four-year-old lab and collie mix. They picked up Corey, the thirty-year-old dishwasher from Lilly's summer work, and headed towards Anchorage International. On the way they dropped Ignatius at Karen's place in Eagle River, where he would have room to run and Karen's mutts for winter company.   At the airport curb Tom left the truck running and gave Corey the house key and a rundown on restarting the furnace. He added a last-minute request not to burn the place to the ground.

"I'll do my best," Corey said with no hint of playfulness. Everyone loved Corey, but he wasn't without history.

They flew first to her parents' place in Arcata, and then over the solid browns of Eastern Wyoming to Casper for his family. Lilly and Tom enjoyed the second fall that came with traveling south while their families ensured they were both still in one piece and overfed them constantly, hoping a few extra pounds would spell safety. Tom's mom warned how Hemorrhagic Dengue Fever was rampant down there—she'd read so on the Center for Disease Control website. They promised to get shots but instead spent the afternoon at a movie they'd seen ads for all summer but never found the time to drive into Anchorage and watch. They put Band-Aids on their arms afterwards to complete the ruse. Tom laughed harder than he had in months and Lilly noticed. They flew to Denver the next morning, then Chicago and on to San Juan that night. Lilly left her Band-Aid on the whole way for luck.

They first learned of the island a year earlier when spending a weekend at a lodge down by Homer at summer's end. The well pump had gone out on a Friday night, with the handyman gone for the weekend. Tom spent five hours fixing it. The couple who owned the lodge thanked him continuously while Lilly insisted that was Tom's ideal vacation. Tom and Lilly refused their offer to drop the cost of one night's stay and began a postcard friendship for the winter. The couple sent some scenic cards from their winter home on the island, suggesting Tom and Lilly come visit. In full hibernation, Tom and Lilly had graciously declined.

Buried among the concerned calls, messages and e-mails of the last two months was a card from the lodge owners. The couple didn't plan on going to the island that winter, leaving their house free, and they felt it was exactly what Lilly and Tom needed. Just pay the utilities, make any needed repairs and keep people from breaking in. It scared Lilly how fast Tom agreed. He didn't say much more about it, but he was very quiet in those weeks. Lilly had gone to the library for books on pirates and sunken treasure.

They spent a night in the San Juan casinos and flew to the island the next day. Lilly liked how the fat clouds hung heavy against the hills and kept the sun from getting out of line. A thick shower rolled over the small airport soon after they landed and sent pilot and passengers alike sprinting inside for cover. Water ran thick off everything and Lilly felt good. It rained in paradise, too.

A *publico* cab in the form of a late 70's van carried them over the island's spine to the south shore and on to the small house. They opened all the windows and let the trade winds do their job. Tom found two tarantulas while unpacking—one dead in the tub, one not so dead in an empty drawer. They went to the market to buy sandals and stock up on familiar food. The house had a phone, but the lines remained down from hurricane season. The lines would not be fixed for another two months, and an additional month would pass before Tom and Lilly noticed.

They bought some terrible-tasting local beer in small cans and sat out on the porch at sunset. They ate name brand frozen pizzas, not wanting to be too brave at first. Rain drifted in over what Tom guessed to be St. Croix in the distance. The shower would hit them eventually, but they enjoyed the sun for now. They talked about how back home the dustings on the mountains would be getting heavier everyday and folks were getting familiar with the winter satellite schedule. Puddles would now crack underfoot and the car started a little harder when leaving the bar at two a.m.

It was good to get Tom talking again. In the past, he could be a real chatterbox once you got him going. Lilly hoped all this would get him talking about a lot of things. Still, she thought, watching the far off rain, even if he didn't, that would be okay, too.

Tom and Lilly awoke at odd hours the first week, the fault of jet lag and local roosters with no circadian rhythms. The birds were fighting roosters, said the neighbor who trained them. These were not time clocks, but rather their own bosses. Tom and Lilly could respect that and let the roosters blend in with the coqui frogs and the electric hum of the cicadas.

After a few days of walking they decided to rent a car and look around. The island's lone rental car fleet, owned by a sly local named Sammy, offered only diminutive Suzuki Samurais.

"Didn't these get outlawed or something up in the states?" Tom asked.

"They just couldn't handle it up there," Sammy said. "That's how everyone else ends up here."

The stripped-down white number they rented came to a rough and ratcheting stop forty-five minutes into the day. Tom borrowed a few tools from a nearby house and fixed the Samurai sufficiently for an afternoon of touring and a return to Sammy. The business owner nodded at their tale.

"That's been happening all month," he said. "I can't

believe you got it fixed."

Sammy didn't drop the rental fee but gave them the white Samurai for a steal and offered Tom a job fixing whatever his gringo renters might break over the winter. Tom promised to show up first thing Monday morning.

"Eighty-thirtyish," Sammy said. "Maybe nine, or ten."

Lilly found work tending bar at the Shipwreck, an open-air bar near the waterfront. It boasted a clientele equal parts year-rounders and tourists and a big screen TV the locals watched from lawn chairs across the street with coolers of cheap beer. After her first night of work they walked the beach sharing a bottle of wine so sweet their fillings ached.

They felt better, somewhat established. They had jobs, didn't need a map and knew where to find a good late breakfast. It had been years since they were new to anywhere, and with their house and circle of friends back home, they were part of the local color to be absorbed.

It's not too late yet, she remembered someone telling her recently. With Tom's thirty-six and her thirty-four there was still time. She wondered exactly when *it's not too late* had replaced *might as well do it while you're young*. Lilly couldn't recall what it wasn't too late for, but figured she and Tom would find out when it rolled around.

Parker was a man with no regrets. A retired aerospace engineer, he'd been wintering on the island for five years and fancied himself, like his drinking companions, a cyclical expatriate who retained complete allegiance. Whenever the F-14's from the Navy base across the water roared low overhead, Parker reminded all present how as a young man the military had wanted him as an aviator. He declined, saying how monkeys could fly airplanes but not design them. He'd helped the owner of the Shipwreck with a loan a couple years back, and while he claimed no ownership, he kept a close if bloodshot eye on his investment.

"You kids been to the caves, Lilly?" he asked one night. Tom, done with work and in for dinner, sat a few stools away.

"The caves at Navio Beach?" she asked.

"Those are the ones, just down the road. You guys been there at high tide?"

Tom shrugged. "We were there, but I don't recall where

the tide was."

Parker tapped his glass on the counter. He closed an eye and tried aiming his remaining good one at both of them.

"Well, go there at high tide, get in the cave and knock one out. I mean just get it on like wild dogs."

Lilly grinned while refilling his Jack and Coke.

"Trust me," Parker said. "You get to pumping away and the waves are just pounding with you. Pounding and *pounding*."

The final syllables set Parker's stool rocking. He grabbed the bar for support and found Lilly's hand.

"Trust me," he said again. "I know."

Lilly shared a glance with Tom, who simply smiled. A person only needed to spend five minutes with Parker to realize he wasn't worth jealousy. In Lilly's one-month tenure at the Shipwreck, Tom had spent five minutes with Parker a hundred times over.

"We'll have to try that," Lilly assured him.

They called their families for Thanksgiving from a payphone off the main road near the water. They talked about their jobs and the house and days spent at the beach and sunburns. Her folks laughed when she told of a mongoose scurrying only ten feet from the phone as they spoke.

Everyone asked if they were doing okay. They both said yes, they were having fun and adapting. Then their families pressed—yes, but is everything *okay*? Tom got off the phone politely but quickly when this started. He tossed rocks into the nearby surf while Lilly wrapped things up.

Things were good, she told them, good as could be expected.

All parties finally realized this was all they would get. These things just take time, Tom's mom said. Lilly said she agreed and hung up, not knowing if Tom's mom was right. Tom could fix anything and always had in the eight years she'd loved him. If something could stop working, Tom could get it going again. It just took effort—a quiet and wordless effort he sunk happily into until whatever needed fixing—a sink, a winch or a generator— was fixed. Tom didn't understand how time might fix things. A dead lawnmower given a few weeks to think would still be just as broken. So on those nights when Tom didn't talk much and seemed a hundred miles away, she could only hope that's where he was—thinking, working, and fixing something.

"Did I ever tell you kids about the time I almost caught the Isla Verde Rapist?"

Parker was the only legitimate customer left in the Shipwreck. Tom sat waiting for Lilly, who cleaned the bar with exaggerated effort hoping Parker might catch the hint.

He continued unprovoked. "I was in San Juan for the weekend, visiting a lady friend. She lived close to the latest attack and wanted a man around. We were coming home from lunch in the Condado one day and heard this yelling and screaming, a real ruckus. A guy came hauling ass out of this little barrio bar full-tilt. Some people inside recognized him from a police sketch in the *San Juan Star* that week. Hell, I knew it was him. He hit the beach and I took off after him. I pulled my .45 from the back of my trunks…"

"You had a gun in your shorts?" Tom said.

Parker's look suggested such behavior was the norm for retired aerospace employees.

"Welcome to the third world, Nanook," Parker said. "So we're tearing across the sand, and there's a good amount of people out that day. When I think I got him, I draw a bead on his upper torso."

Parker aimed an imaginary pistol at Tom.

"But before I can shoot, the whole damn beach jumps to their feet, freaking out. I still saw him, but with everyone standing I couldn't guarantee a clean shot." Parker lowered his hands. "So I didn't shoot. I don't do something if I don't know going into it how things will turn out. That's when mistakes happen."

Lilly stopped wiping the counter top.

"You were ready for that?" she said. "To shoot him?"

"Oh yeah. It's not so hard." Parker tapped his temple. "It's all a mindset. The trigger finger becomes just another mechanism."

Lilly looked to Tom, who clinked the ice in his water glass in small circles.

"You know Duff, right?" Parker said.

They both nodded. The fit grey-haired man lived on a twenty-five foot Catalina anchored not a hundred feet off the nearby waterfront. Its position lights were visible from the bar. Duff rowed in most mornings and took off on his bike to a hammock in Navio Cove. There he read, wrote and apparently watched Parker pound away in the caves, tides willing.

"The retired sporting goods guy, right?" Lilly said.

Parker dismissed her with a sloppy wave.

"That's a bullshit story. I have it on good authority that he was a marksman, a shootist." He took a quick drink to let his insinuations sink in. "That's right—an assassin."

"For who?" Tom said.

Parker smiled. "The government, man. CIA, FBI, maybe some outfit we never heard of. Deep, deep undercover, kid. Real Robert Ludlum shit."

Lilly turned off the big screen. The sports highlights died with a hum and the locals across the street began packing up their lawn chairs.

"Did he...*do* anyone we've every heard of?"

"Maybe, maybe not," Parker said. "He probably offed a lot of folks before Johnny Q ever heard about them. Preventative maintenance of sorts."

Tom laughed. "What's he doing down here?"

Parker shook his head. "He's obviously been deactivated, sent here and given a new name and all that. He'll give you that sporting goods line 'til he's blue in the face, but look in his eyes next time he's in for dinner. You'll see. He knows what he's done and isn't at peace. He's calm and cool but that don't mean it's all sitting right."

Parker pointed to the Shipwreck's outdoor barbeque pit.

"Last winter one of them Navy SEAL teams was out here for maneuvers. They asked to use the pit for a barbeque. Despite what you see in movies, this was the best-behaved group of boys I've ever seen. They drank a few beers, but they might as well have been a church group. Everything was 'yes, ma'am,' or 'no, sir.' They kept completely to themselves. They'd done things, you could tell.

"So Duff came in that night, and I saw something. He seemed off at first, noticing them SEALs, but then relaxed. No one said anything, but each knew the other's story. A kindred spirits thing."

Parker put his glass on the counter and, for the first time in Lilly's memory, left of his own accord.

"Watch your backs, kids," he said descending the stairs. "These parts are full of histories."

One night Tom didn't come in for dinner. Lilly returned home to find him very drunk with only one light on and the radio silent. She asked if he wanted it on.

"There's nothing but happy music down here," he said.

Lilly knew the little radio was lucky to still be in one piece. Tom was a good man and a fixer at heart, but had taken a few things apart in his past.

"It's all Grateful Dead out of St. Thomas or upbeat dance crap from San Juan. Ricky Martin or that Elvis Crespo."

Lilly sat next to him, knowing better than to take his hand.

"I might have a Johnny Cash tape somewhere in my bag."

Tom thought about it, though the house didn't have a cassette player. He finally shook his head.

"It wouldn't fit."

He talked for a while as Lilly listened. He talked about home, how the cold and rain let a person be sad and still feel welcome. A person could be happy there, too, but it was a good place to be down and feel in good company.

"I guess that's the draw of these places," Lilly said. "It's harder to stay sad."

Tom stood and said he didn't think that was right. A person had a right to hurt and feel at home. She couldn't argue. He kissed her forehead, said he loved her and opened the glass door to the deck. He told her how there were stars in that night sky they wouldn't see after the spring and he was going to get an eyeful. She gave him a half-hour alone and then joined him. He sat in a plastic chair, smelling of Don Q and sea air. Without looking back he held out his hand. She took it and tried to find what star he was looking at. His eyes hung low, as if not looking at the sky, but rather the beacons of the boats in the small bay.

Tom and Lilly had seen Duff plenty of times and talked on occasion, but nothing stood out in their memories. A person only gave so much attention to interactions with someone who pushed sneakers and tank tops for twenty years. Now they watched for him everywhere—on the roads, at the beach, and in the market. They didn't talk about their new shared interest, but both took each sighting—even one as expected as Duff's regular bike rides out to Navio—with the thrill of Bigfoot or a black wolf. They waved and he waved back, flashing a sweaty smile. They imagined him decades younger in bushes and trees around the world's various upstart countries, biding his time and waiting for a clean shot. In his crosshairs rested the enemy. Tom saw revolutionaries in fatigues and berets, maybe even a cigar *a la* Castro. Lilly envisioned slick, well-dressed drug lords of vaguely South American descent, direct from *Miami Vice*. Whoever they were they never knew what hit them, walking with bodyguards one minute and dropping like a sack of hammers the next. All of them must have had it coming. Tom and Lilly only needed to look into the blue-grey crystals of Duff's eyes to know. Otherwise Duff wouldn't be able to cope. A man couldn't kill like Duff had—numbering now in the hundreds in their collective imagination—and still manage to hit the Shipwreck every Tuesday for free appetizers with New England snowbirds unless he knew some secret.

Three days before Christmas they started up the island's longest grade and found Duff walking with four plastic market bags. Their next action felt inevitable.

Duff climbed over the Samurai's tailgate and thanked them, calling Tom "Tim" and Lilly simply "Hon." He offered them each a Malta India from his bag and started one himself.

"Stolen," he said through a mouthful when Lilly asked about his otherwise omnipresent bike.

"Do you know who took it?" Tom said.

Duff nodded. "I've got a pretty good idea, but it's not really worth pursuing. Small island, y'know. Not worth making an enemy."

"Still," Lilly said. "It's your bike."

Duff agreed with a shrug. "Yeah, I know, but we're a contained system here. It'll make its way around to me. I'll just steal it back next time I see it."

After a few miles Duff asked Tom to stop for a minute near a rusted wire fence where a Calabash tree encroached on the road's shoulder. Without leaving the backseat Duff craned his neck to study what he could see of the land beyond. He then tapped Tom's shoulder and bid him to carry on.

"That land's for sale," Duff said. "I'm considering throwing in a bid."

"Giving up the boat?" Lilly said.

"Oh, I'll keep it, but I want a little of my own dirt under my feet. Settle down, y'know, maybe some animals."

Tom smiled. "Chickens and hogs and such?"

Duff dropped his empty bottle in the bag. "You guys ever heard of fainting goats?"

Neither of them had so Duff spent the next couple miles explaining Tennessee fainting goats. While similar in appearance to other goats, when startled this breed's muscles would lock up and cause them to fall over, or faint. Duff ended with a pantomime of a goat in action, his arms stuck out arthritically in a mock faint.

"Not exactly Old MacDonald's farm," Lilly said.

Duff grinned. "No, but I like their style. Things get a little too crazy, they drop down and take a break."

"How long are they out for?" Lilly said.

"Depends. This is me up here, kid." Duff signaled at the boardwalk where his tender was tied below. "Some five seconds, some thirty. However long it takes to get their bearings straight."

Tom eased the Suzuki onto the dirt shoulder, allowing a *publico* to tear past. Silent since the mention of fainting goats, he turned to Duff.

"Did you really do all those things?" he asked. "All those people?"

Lilly delivered a silencing punch. Tom took it and just waited for Duff's answer.

Duff laughed like he'd just made a screaming deal on medicine balls or jump ropes. He hopped over the tailgate and pulled out his plastic bags, grinning at the dirt.

"Well, Tim, contrary to public opinion, the sporting goods game isn't quite that cutthroat. It never went that far."

"Duff, I apologize," Lilly started. Duff only laughed again and waved off her concern.

"Unnecessary, sweetie. With nothing but Spanish TV I realize there's not much to do but listen to Parker and his cronies for entertainment. I'm guilty, myself."

"I was wrong to ask," Tom said, though without remorse.

Duff shook his head and smiled. "Not at all. Just tell

Parker I didn't faint, and to watch himself. I might just come out of retirement."

Duff made his right hand into a pistol, aimed far above their heads, and pulled the trigger without hesitation.

"I'll see you kids on Tuesday night for the free *hors d'oeuvres*."

Tom and Lilly waved and Duff made his way down the rocky beachfront to his tender.

It was three days into January and Parker had been drinking since noon. He either didn't want the previous year to end or was trying to jumpstart the new one. A few other regulars hung in a loose orbit about him, surrendering occasionally to the big screen's gravitational pull. Lilly was taking her dinner break with Tom at the bar near the door. The trades blew light and the day's dying sky suggested a new year's hope.

"Of course he's going to deny it and make jokes," Parker said. "Jesus, kids, the fucking government trained him to do that. It's gullibility like yours that keeps them in power."

Tom shrugged. Lilly had been babysitting the now-slurring Parker six hours and was considering calling Duff about free-lance rates.

"He is not a man at peace," Parker said.

"He seemed pretty peaceful," Tom said. "Whatever he did."

"An act." Parker took a long pull of Heineken. "Hell, I don't know what'd be harder to come to terms with—doing in all those people or spending your life pushing jockstraps."

This set loose an inner chuckle that rocked Parker from his stool. He tumbled halfway down the stool before catching himself. His green bottle flew across the room, shattering at the feet of Louie, a PRT repairman whose girth threatened the integrity of the island's telephone poles. The big man eyed his friend Parker with anger first, then a lazy understanding. He kicked the larger shards away and returned to the soccer match on the big screen.

Parker cursed and made a feeble attempt to stand, failing and winding up again hanging on the stool.

"Jesus, Parker," Lilly said. She took a dustpan for the glass while Tom attended to Parker.

"I'm fine," Parker insisted. "Fucking fine."

"No argument here," Tom said. He got a good purchase under Parker's bony arms and stood him up. "It's only the third of January, man, not too late for a resolution or two."

Parker shook his head and attempted composure. "I don't make resolutions. If I want to do something, I do it. And I damn sure don't do things just 'cause we went around the sun one more time."

"Fair enough," Tom said.

"Maybe your slacker generation can catch on someday," Parker said. "You have to *do* things. Things don't just happen."

On this last syllable, Parker moved into Tom. Maybe he lunged, maybe he fell, but the end result was the old man's unshaven face coming to rest in Tom's t-shirt and his leathery hand hitting Tom's stomach. Tom fell backwards but quickly regained his footing. He dragged Parker up with one hand under the man's armpit, the other hand free to do what it may.

Lilly hadn't seen Tom in a brawl in years, but she recognized this immediately as a lopsided match. She waited for Tom's free hand to roundabout and find Parker's face, asking the arrogant nobody how this all fit into his plan, how he himself had somehow planned this, and made it happen. She no longer waited, but now *wanted* Tom's fist to show Parker how accidents were real, and sometimes things just happened.

The errant hand instead found Parker's other armpit and hoisted the man surely to his sandaled feet. Tom gave Lilly a smile and laugh that took back the last three days and started her year all over again. Parker hung onto Tom, slurring so much the words defied either apology or threat. Only half the bar's customers gave the exchange any attention, and they went back to the soccer match when a peaceful resolution seemed inevitable. Tom led Parker towards the door.

"He's all right," Tom assured Lilly. "He just overdid himself a bit. I'll run him home. Give him a little while, he'll be back to normal soon."

He kissed Lilly's cheek and the two men disappeared down the front steps.

Tom and Lilly weren't sure exactly when Duff got his bike back, but they saw him riding in long green socks on St.

Patrick's Day. The land he wanted sold to a Montauk couple who were planning another guesthouse, but Duff wasn't too upset and even stopped to greet them with a shout of faith and begora. The fainting goats still occupied his mind. Maybe he would just buy some and set them free on the island. Anywhere else they wouldn't last, but Duff felt they'd be okay there.

They stopped by the payphone a week later and called their house. Corey assured them that despite frozen pipes and a territorial winter moose, all was in order. The furnace worked fine and they were through the worst of things for now. He asked when they were coming back.

"Probably not as early as we thought," Tom said. "Not this spring. Maybe not all summer."

Corey was silent in consideration. If Alaska was a board game, starting summer was passing "Go." Miss it and you might as well not even play.

"You think you can keep our place from burning to the ground one more season?"

"I can try," Corey said. "Take it month by month."

Tom watched Lilly, her pant legs rolled up and wading in the nearby surf, and assured Corey that would be good enough.

MARCEL JOLLEY was born and raised in Skagway, Alaska. He lives in the Pacific Northwest with his wife, Cathy, and son, Will.

Black Lawrence Press

Contemporary Literature

www.blacklawrencepress.com

Because there's no such thing as
TOO MANY BOOKS.